FINDING COMFORT

CHRISTINE GAEL

INTRODUCTION

Stephanie Ketterman's only daughter, Sarah, thought her days living in Bluebird Bay were over. Married only two years, living in Washington DC, and on the cusp of an amazing career in law, she had the next decade planned out to a T. When she suddenly realizes she is bitterly unhappy and may have left Bluebird Bay in order to escape the pain of losing her father at such a young age, she returns.

Solo.

Can she tear it all down and build something new...something that truly brings her joy, or will her fear of failing again keep her from even trying to find happiness?

Fallyn Rappaport has tried her darnedest not to let David Shaw pull her back into the world of investigating, but she's finding it harder and harder to say no. Both to the juicy new case he is working on, and to David himself...

1

SARAH

"This counter space, though!" Sarah exclaimed as she pulled salad fixings from a brown paper bag. The kitchen in her brother's new rental was gorgeous, with wide counters and a huge gas range.

Todd grinned. "Not bad, huh?"

"Not bad, he says!" She bumped him out of the way with her hip to go fumbling through his cabinets for a salad bowl. They were a mess, Tupperware and pots all piled together. Typical.

"Looking for this?" Todd said. She looked up to see him holding the bowl she had been searching for.

"Yes. Thank you. And this place would cost over, like, three grand a month in some parts of DC."

"Good thing we're not in DC," Todd laughed. "I would never want to pay that much for a one bedroom. That's nuts."

"But it's a *nice* one bedroom," Sarah told him. It was at least twice the size of her place, and the kitchen was worlds better than the one she had been making do with.

"I could get something nicer, but Alice and I are saving up for a house."

"So soon?" said Sarah without thinking. Todd shot her a glare, and she glanced away.

She was the last person to be counseling him on love right now. She and Oliver had been together for years before they moved in together, and look at them now.

Shifting her thoughts, she looked over her ingredients. Olive oil, balsamic, honey, liquid smoke...she'd had to get it all because Todd's fridge and pantry were decked out in true bachelor style. Ketchup, mustard, and leftover Chinese food. None of the basic staples to make tonight's dressing. She couldn't complain. It was a free place to stay, and hey, at least the guy had a blender for his morning smoothies.

"We don't have a joint bank account or anything," Todd muttered. "We're each saving on our own. A down payment will take a while — though maybe not as long as I'd thought. The clinic is doing better than ever since bringing in part-time help, and Alice doesn't pay her aunt any rent. Anyway, by the time we have enough money, we'll know for sure if we want to try living together."

Sarah could tell by her brother's tone — not to mention the way he looked at Alice — that he was already surer than sure. But she didn't press.

"You should see what passes for a kitchen in DC," she said lightly. "About four square feet of counter space to work with and an electric stove that takes ten minutes to boil enough water for tea. I hate it."

"So move," Todd said easily. "You never liked it there anyway."

"It wasn't all bad," Sarah murmured.

Todd raised an eyebrow at her, then smiled and shrugged. She wasn't sure what to make of this easygoing, happy-go-lucky new Todd. He had always been almost as Type A as she was, completely dedicated to veterinary school and then taking their mother's veterinary clinic to the next level after the death of their father. But ever since Alice came into his life, stress and worry seemed to roll right off of him. She couldn't even imagine what that was like.

Sarah frowned and turned her attention back to the dressing she was making. She chopped an apple into rough pieces and tossed it into a blender, then topped it with the spices she had gathered at the grocery store. But try as she might to focus, she couldn't shake her brother's comment about leaving her apartment. Sarah had been bending Todd's ear for months about her floundering marriage, had even called him crying the day she filed for divorce. But she hadn't fully moved out of the apartment that she shared with Oliver.

Not yet.

Her transient position as a law clerk at a firm in DC had wrapped up nearly two weeks ago. Before driving up to Maine for their aunt's wedding, Sarah had spent a full week doing *nothing* instead of packing all her stuff.

That had been a first for her. Ever since childhood, she had been something of an overachiever. She enjoyed challenges and accomplishing things. But these days?

She was just tired.

It had been so nice to have the tiny apartment all to herself while Oliver was at work all day. She would need to make the move soon, but they'd ended things amicably, and Oliver wasn't rushing her.

For the first time in her life, she felt unsure...hesitant to take that next step, even though her time in Bluebird Bay had convinced her that this was where she wanted to be.

What if she made another mistake?

"Did I tell you about Aunt Anna and Barnaby?" Todd could read a room, bless him. He hadn't objected when Sarah had chosen to sleep on his couch rather than staying in their family home with their mother, Stephanie. He hadn't asked intrusive questions. He just let her be most of the time... and occasionally regaled her with animal stories from the clinic when he thought she could use a pick-me-up.

Her brother launched into a story about Anna trying to buy the macaw's love with a new toy, but Sarah wasn't really listening. She put the salad together on autopilot: arugula, endives, apples...usually she candied the pecans, but today she just dumped them straight into the salad bowl.

The hanger steak Todd had bought started to sizzle and steam as he dropped it into his huge cast-iron pan, and the kitchen filled with the appetizing smell of seared meat.

Their phones sounded in unison, both buzzing loudly as they vibrated on the kitchen island, and Sarah paused to check hers.

"Mom's on her way over," she told Todd. It was supposedly Sarah's last night in town – as far as their mother knew, anyway – and she had promised herself that she would come clean to her about what she had been hiding for months.

The slow, painful disintegration of her marriage, just two years in.

Sarah had fielded a dozen questions about Oliver when she showed up to her aunt's wedding solo. And, while she didn't exactly lie about his whereabouts, she didn't tell the whole truth, either. No one but Todd and Jeff knew that Sarah had filed for divorce weeks ago, or that sleeping on Todd's couch for a few days was a breeze after sleeping on the couch in her own home for the past *six months*.

She had wanted to turn to her mother when everything started to fall apart. Of course she had. But between Dad dying and *Pop* dying and Jeff dropping out of school and Mom developing a dependency on prescription painkillers... she just couldn't add her failure of a marriage to the mix. She hadn't wanted to pile on... or try to explain how brutally hard it felt simply being married to a nice guy. If there were words for that, Sarah still hadn't found them.

And she was usually good with words. It was kind of her thing.

If Oliver had cheated on her, it would have been easy to leave.

If he were abusive, everyone would understand.

And those very thoughts were what made Sarah realize that she couldn't stay. Day in and day out, living with this bland, easygoing man she had promised to love for all of eternity... she found herself daydreaming that he would give her an out — that he would do something just heinous enough for her to feel justified in burning their marriage to the ground.

Of course, he never did. Oliver was a good guy. Intelligent, quiet, thoughtful.

He hadn't even reacted when she told him that she wanted out... and she supposed that was part of the problem. He was no more passionate about Sarah than she was about him. He was just more complacent... more willing to keep going along as they were, with their lukewarm friendship masquerading as marriage.

"At least we like each other," he said the first time she tried to talk to him about what she was feeling. "It's not so bad."

And that had been enough to shut Sarah up for two more months. Between work and volunteering, she was hardly home anyway. Oliver was the world's easiest roommate, clean and courteous. Maybe he was right. Maybe it was enough that they didn't hate each other.

But slowly, the whisper in her mind grew to a roar that drowned out everything else.

Leave, it told her. *You both deserve better than "It's not so bad."*

And *still*, something held her back. The fears that pinned her in place were elusive and slippery. She knew that she could live alone. She knew that she could get a new job or start her own practice anywhere she liked. She knew that there were more fish in the sea.

So *what* was she so afraid of?

Sarah poured in the various liquids and switched the blender on high, letting the roar of the motor drown out her thoughts. When she turned it off again, she said to Todd, "Maybe we can just put it off for another day. I'm not supposed to leave until tomorrow, and there's no point in rushing things. I can talk to her at brunch tomorrow, or call her from—"

Todd put a stop to her blabbering with the sort of look that only a sibling can manage.

"You're a grownup, Sarah. Mom will understand. You won't be the first person to get a divorce, you know."

"I'm aware," Sarah grumbled.

People got divorced every day. But people also drove drunk and flunked out of algebra and dropped out of law school. She had never been one of *those* people.

The truth was, she felt like a failure. And aside from raw onions, the thing she hated most — the thing that she had successfully avoided nearly every day of her life — was failing.

Speaking of which…

Sarah swooped in and pulled her salad bowl out of the way just before Todd dumped in a pile of raw onions. On top of the apples and pecans. Like an animal.

"You're the steak guy," she told him. "Don't mess with my salad."

"But I have all this onion left over," Todd said, sounding for a moment like the whiny kid she remembered from childhood. "If I put any more in the pan, they won't caramelize right."

"That sounds like a 'you' problem." Sarah put a protective plate over the top of the salad bowl. Todd rolled his eyes and turned to check on the steak. He spluttered in protest as she dumped the rest of the onions into the second frying pan. Sarah ignored him and ripped open a bag of dried cranberries.

"Hello!" Steph called as she walked through the front door. "It smells amazing in here!"

"Hi Mom!" Sarah went to hug Steph as she walked into the kitchen. "How was class?"

"It was fun! I taught two beginners classes in a row this afternoon — a normal one and a chair-based one for older folks. I was skeptical when they offered it to me, but I think now it's my favorite one."

"Steak's done!" Todd announced, putting it on a cutting board. "Just needs to sit for a few before I cut into it. I'm just gonna jump in and out of the shower. Oh, and Sarah has some news to share."

Sarah turned to him with a wide-eyed look of betrayal, and he responded with the exact grin he used to give her after sneaking into her room and reading her diary.

Brothers.

"What news?" asked Steph pleasantly. Behind her, Todd gave Sarah a melodramatic salute and slipped out of the kitchen.

"Wine, Mom?" Sarah parried, panic clutching at her chest. "He has red and white. But I'm guessing you'll want red with your steak? We didn't make appetizers or anything."

A look of concern came over Steph's face as her daughter babbled. "What's the news, Sarah?"

Sarah let out a heavy sigh and shot a glare in her brother's general direction. Then, she turned to her mom with her best approximation of a smile. "I'm moving back to Bluebird Bay."

"Oh my God! That's wonderful!" Steph exclaimed, pulling her into another hug. "Have you found a place to live already? When is Oliver coming?"

Sarah took a step back, pulse skittering as she swallowed hard. "Um, actually, he's not."

Her mother's smile faltered. "What do you mean?"

Sarah sighed and poured two glasses of wine. Oops, none left for Todd. *Too bad, so sad.*

She took a sip of hers and said, "Oliver and I had been separated for months. I hadn't told anyone yet because I thought that we might work it out... but we've just been living like roommates for so long. And now it's official. We're getting divorced."

"Oh, Sarah, I'm so sorry."

"I'm sorry I didn't say something sooner," Sarah said, staring down at the gray lines on the faux marble counter. "Things have just been so crazy, what with Pop living with you and then, well, *not* living with you, and Jeff moving home... and every time I come to visit there's something big happening, like a funeral or a wedding. The timing just never felt right, and neither did talking about it over the phone."

"It's okay." Steph was trying to soothe her, but Sarah knew her mother well enough to hear the hurt and confusion hiding beneath the concern in her voice. Steph took a sip of her own wine and then asked, "Do you still need to go back and get your stuff? Where will you stay?"

"I brought everything I'll need while I'm here at Todd's place. He said I can stay until I find a place to rent in town. I went to see a couple places this week, but one was all moldy and the other had neighbors fighting upstairs. I'm going to check out some more options in a few days."

Steph was quiet for a long moment, and Sarah knew that her mom was wondering why Sarah hadn't come to stay with her. Sarah didn't know how to explain that it had nothing to do with their relationship. It's just that returning to her childhood bedroom would have felt like the final nail in the coffin of her failed life. She had deliberately chosen the discomfort of Todd's couch over their mother's spacious house to make sure that she wouldn't be floating driftlessly for too long. But she didn't know how to explain that, and her mom didn't ask her to.

After a while, Steph asked, "How is Oliver taking all of this?"

"He's fine," Sarah said, not meeting her mother's eyes. "That's kind of the problem."

"What do you mean?"

"He doesn't much care one way or another. With him, it's always, 'Whatever you say.' And at first I thought that was a good thing, but now... I want someone who *cares* about things, you know? Who cares about *me*. I know this is the right thing for me."

"You know best, sweetheart," her mom said.

Sarah shot her a glance and, while love and concern were written on her mother's face, there was also a hint of doubt. That hurt more than Sarah wanted to admit.

"Ready to eat?" Todd asked as he walked back into the kitchen with wet hair and fresh clothes. "I'm starved."

"Sure," said Steph. Her voice was still unsteady, but she mustered up a smile for her golden child. "Thank you for making dinner. It smells amazing."

"I made salad," Sarah said, and immediately felt embarrassed of herself. Childish. The too-sunny smile her mother gave her only intensified that feeling.

"Thank you, sweetheart. It looks great. Let's eat."

Todd's eyebrows rose when he picked up the bottle of merlot and discovered that it was empty. Steph was busy setting the table, and Sarah stuck her tongue out at her brother. He chuckled, shook his head, and pulled a fresh bottle of wine from a cupboard above the refrigerator.

Her big brother was her favorite person in the whole world... and the one most likely to drive her to acts of violence. Family was weird like that.

Once they were seated at the table, serving up their salad and topping it with slices of steak, Steph summoned up some words of encouragement for her daughter.

"Everything will work out, Sarah. You'll see. You're brilliant and strong and you'll figure this out. It's all going to be okay."

Sarah looked up at her mom and forced a smile. "I know."

But when she dropped her eyes back to her plate, she felt unsure.

Sarah had taken the safe route with Oliver. They had gotten married because their relationship felt easy and stable. There was no drama. No red flags. At least, none that she had recognized.

Oliver was kind and smart and affable.

And she *still* couldn't hack it. She had blown up a marriage with a perfectly nice guy, and in less than two years. Divorced in her mid-twenties. What did that say about *her*?

Only one word came to mind, playing on a loop in her head, and it wasn't onions.

It was failure.

2

CEE-CEE

CEE-CEE CARRIED her unfrosted cupcakes upstairs one tray at a time. Usually she frosted them down in the basement kitchen around six in the morning — but this evening Mick and Jeff were working after hours, and Cee-cee figured she would take advantage of the company. It would give her a chance to sleep in tomorrow morning; she could come down when the shop opened at eight instead of getting up at four to bake like she usually did. She also had one round of cupcakes left to frost for a birthday order that was being picked up tonight — the final flavor of the seven colors they had ordered to create a cupcake rainbow.

Mick grinned at Cee-cee as she set the cupcakes down and began piping swirls of frosting onto each one. She felt a flurry of butterflies that had never faded, even after Mick had moved into her apartment and become a part of her daily life. She couldn't believe her good luck in sharing her golden years with this marvelous man, and she didn't think that feeling would ever fade.

After their wedding, Mick and Cee-cee made the most of

their short honeymoon by going to a swanky resort and spa up the coast. Three days of couples massages, eucalyptus-scented saunas, and long walks on the beach. They feasted on gourmet food every night and — perhaps the most decadent thing of all — lounged in bed for hours every morning. Now that they were back home in Bluebird Bay, they were determined to bring a little bit of that luxury into their everyday life. They might not have a personal sauna, but some things were within reach: relaxed mornings, delicious food, and long walks in nature would all be a part of their quotidian life together.

Cee-cee could hardly believe that she and Mick had only been married for a week. All of the nerves and work leading up to the wedding, and yet the day itself had passed them by in the blink of an eye. Maybe it was because they had been living together for some time now, but Cee-cee felt like she and Mick had been married for months already. She couldn't imagine what her life would look like without him — and she didn't want to.

"Slide it back just a bit," Mick said to Jeff, and the heavy piece of wood they were holding fell into place. "Perfect."

They were installing a new butcher-block countertop, one of Mick's wedding presents to Cee-cee. It would make good use of a small bit of wasted space behind the counter in the cupcake shop. It was a space that Cee-cee and her employees would be able to use to add last-minute inscriptions and custom toppings.

She loved watching her husband and her nephew working together. Jeff was thriving under Mick's gentle guidance, and Cee-cee was so grateful they had each other. Mick had a good relationship with Max and Gabe, but he would never truly know what it was like to have children of his own. And Jeff had been so lost after losing his father and grandfather in rapid succession. They each filled a gap for the other, and it was beautiful to see their relationship grow.

"You know Jeff picked the wood for this?" said Mick, shooting Cee-cee a smile. "He's got a real eye for raw materials. Like Michelangelo seeing statues trapped in blocks of stone."

"The Michelangelo of wood," Cee-cee said with a grin. "I like it."

"I don't know about that," Jeff protested, blushing slightly.

"Are you good to finish up here?" Mick asked. "It just needs to be cleaned and oiled, and then you can pack everything up."

Cee-cee smiled and looked down at the bright red frosting she was piping onto cupcakes. Jeff was saving up for a new car, and Mick went out of his way to give him extra hours to help him save all that he could.

"Yeah, I can do that," Jeff said.

Mick walked over to where Cee-cee stood working and bent to kiss her cheek. "Are you almost done here? I can go upstairs and get dinner started."

"Yeah, this is the last tray," she told him. "Amber should be in any minute to pick everything up."

"Great. I'll see you in a few." Mick planted another kiss on her temple and headed upstairs.

"Would it be okay if I put some music on, Aunt Cee-cee?"

She smiled at Jeff. "Go ahead."

He hooked his phone up to the shop's Bluetooth, and Cee-cee immediately regretted her decision. Jeff loved the grating, robotic music that was so popular with his generation. What was it they called that type of music? Autotune? To Cee-cee, it sounded worse than cats yowling in an alley. But at the same time, watching Jeff dance and sing under his breath while he went about his work made her grin. And the beat had her shaking her own hips, even if the machine-altered singing grated on her ears. Just a few more minutes and she could retreat upstairs.

She had started that morning with vibrant purple ube cupcakes, making enough for both the party and the shop, and she was just putting the finishing touches on her newest flavor now: a healthy take on classic red velvet that she called Beet Cute. Both the deep red cakes and the bright red frosting were dyed with beets. The blue cupcakes were the ever-popular butterfly pea, the green were her new eucalyptus mint flavor, the orange were her top-selling Creamsicle cupcakes, and she had used turmeric to turn her lemon frosting a golden yellow. The lemon pound cake was the first recipe she had ever perfected; it had been her mom's favorite. Cee-cee used to make some version of it every year for her birthday.

The thought made her flinch, because it brought The Big Nate Problem to the front of her mind. As much as she tried not to think about it, she couldn't get that memory out of her head: the night that Chaz Bartholomew showed up at her house twenty-five years ago — the night of her mother's birthday party. Which, if memory served, coincided with the night of Emily Addison's disappearance. *The* Chaz Bartholomew who was now in jail, along with his wife

Nancy, awaiting trial for the murder of seventeen-year-old Emily Addison.

Cee-cee didn't want to believe that Nate could have been involved with that heinous crime in any way... but the coincidence was too glaring to ignore. She couldn't shake the memory of how strange Nate had behaved after Chaz dropped by out of the blue. The way he had disappeared for the second half of the party. Or the way he'd been acting the past few weeks. At first, Cee-cee had attributed it to her upcoming wedding, or new financial worries... but once she made the connection to the timing of Emily's disappearance and the recent discovery of her body at the bottom of the bay, Cee-cee had realized that Nate had started acting very strange right around the time that story broke. Could *both* things be pure coincidence? Something in Cee-cee's gut said that there was more to it than that.

She finished icing the last cupcake and looked at Jeff, who was shaking his backside to his terrible, cheerful music as he oiled her new butcher-block counter.

If she stirred the pot and found out that her suspicions were right, what would that do to Max and Gabe? Their father could end up in prison. How could she take Gabe's father from him just weeks after he became a father himself? How could she take Nate from her son the way Jeff's father had been ripped away from him?

Her kids would be furious with her... wouldn't they?

Sure, they weren't as close to Nate as they had once been. But he was still their father. He was a part of them, half of what made them who they were.

And what if Cee-cee was wrong? What if she stirred up a bunch of drama and upset over nothing? Nate wasn't the best of husbands, but surely murder was out of the question.

Wasn't it?

"Well?" Jeff asked, gesturing to the now-gleaming counter with a flourish. "What do you think, Aunt Cee-cee?"

"It looks beautiful, Jeff." Cee-cee pushed away her worries to give her nephew a genuine smile. "And it will give me so much more room to work without having to go up and down the stairs every five minutes. Thank you."

The bell above the door sounded and Cee-cee turned, expecting to see Amber here to pick up her cupcakes. Instead, her sister Stephanie walked in with a fearful scowl on her face. Cee-cee could almost see a cartoon storm cloud above her head, raging with thunder and lightning.

"Did *you* know about this?" she exclaimed as the door swung shut behind her.

"About what?" Cee-cee asked.

"Sarah's getting a divorce. Apparently, she and Oliver split *six months ago* and I'm only hearing about it now."

"Ohhh poor Sarah," Cee-cee murmured, thinking back to the last time she had seen her niece. She had seemed happy enough at Cee-cee's wedding, but of course Cee-cee had been so distracted. And she had *definitely* asked about Oliver; Sarah had evaded the question somehow, and Cee-cee hadn't even noticed. She felt like a heel.

Steph jabbed her finger at Jeff. "Did you know about Sarah and Oliver?"

Jeff looked away before nodding sheepishly.

"Is everyone keeping secrets from me, for crying out loud?"

"Whoa, chill out, Mom! I just found out," Jeff said,

holding up a defensive hand. "She didn't want to upstage Aunt Cee-cee on her big day. And she didn't want to upset you, not after—"

"I'm fine!" Steph shouted. She took a deep breath and tried again. "I'm fine. I'm not upset about Sarah and Oliver splitting up. If that's what's best for her, it's fine. And I am so excited to have her moving back to Bluebird Bay—"

"Sarah's moving home?" Cee-cee interrupted. "That's wonderful! I mean, sad about her and Oliver, but..."

"Yes, it's wonderful. It's fine. It's fine and it's wonderful," Steph said in a rush, very clearly *not* fine. "I'm not angry about her divorce. But I'm hurt that all *three* of my children felt that they had to hide this from me!"

Jeff frowned. "I'm sorry you feel betrayed but it wasn't my news to share, Mom."

"I just can't believe Sarah didn't feel like she could talk to me. She's been going through this for months — and we talk all the time! And still she never breathed a word of it." Steph slumped into one of the chairs that lined the front of the shop. "I feel like I failed her, Cee-cee."

Cee-cee wanted to wrap her sister in a hug, but Steph didn't look like she was in a hugging mood. "Do you want a cupcake?"

"No, I don't want a *cupcake*. I want this family to stop treating me like I'm going to break! I developed a short-lived dependency on extremely addictive prescription drugs after I lost my husband and almost got murdered. But I'm okay now. I haven't had a single slipup. Not even when I had Pop living with me, for crying out loud. Do you know how stressful that was?"

"I know, Steph," Cee-cee said in a soothing voice. "You're doing great."

"I'm not going to break," Steph growled. "The only thing I'm going to crack is some skulls if you all keep tiptoeing around me. Got it?"

Jeff nodded, wide-eyed. This sort of outburst was completely out of character for his mother. It reminded Cee-cee of Steph's teenage years, but she wondered if Steph's children had ever seen her lose it like this. She suspected not — at least, not in a very long time.

"Okay?" Steph pressed.

"*I'm* not tiptoeing around you," Cee-cee told her. "I lean on you. You're my rock."

Steph smiled at that. "Thank you. Then I think I would like a cupcake."

Cee-cee chuckled. "Take your pick."

The door opened again and Amber came rushing in. "Sorry I'm late!" she exclaimed. "It's been a *day*. Is everything ready?"

"Sure is." Cee-cee gestured to the three stacks of boxes next to the register.

"You are a rock star," Amber said, handing Cee-cee a credit card.

They all helped her carry the cupcakes to her car, and then Steph and her youngest headed home. Cee-cee closed up shop and walked upstairs to her apartment, where she was greeted with the smell of caramelized onions and sun-dried tomatoes.

"That smells amazing," she said to Mick.

"Just twenty more minutes and we can eat," he said,

peeking into the oven. He turned off the burner on the stovetop and turned to kiss her.

Cee-cee's shoulders were tight with nerves, and Mick pulled back to give her a questioning look. "Is something wrong?"

Steph's tirade about secrets had filled Cee-cee with the sudden urge to spill it. She didn't want there to be any secrets between herself and her new husband... even if saying all of her worries out loud made her feel like a paranoid fool. She needed to tell Mick what was on her mind.

Cee-cee took a deep breath and said, "I think Nate might have been involved with Emily's disappearance."

3

SARAH

Even though Bluebird Bay was her hometown, this move was going to be a fresh start for Sarah. Her divorce wasn't a failure. Moving home wasn't a *failure*, she reminded herself with a sniff. It was an opportunity to reinvent herself, and she intended to make the most of it.

There was a new health food store in town that hadn't existed when she was growing up, and she spent the morning getting acquainted with it. It was a gorgeous spring day and the store was only a mile away, so she had walked there. Now, she was walking down the street towards her brother's little rental carrying grocery bags chock full of healthy food. She bought zucchini for spiralized noodles and everything she would need to make homemade pesto. There were frozen pouches of acai that she would use to make Instagram-worthy smoothie bowls in the morning before Todd went to work. Even the *snacks* were healthy: coconut chips, dried mango, almond butter and celery... once Sarah was done food prepping, she would walk back across town to her mom's afternoon yoga class. That would be four miles in one day *and...* whatever it was that people did in yoga classes. Sarah had never been to one. But it was time to find out! The class was both a stepping stone on her path to vibrant good health and a peace offering to her mother after months of secrets and half-truths.

Say hello to Sarah two-point-oh! Sarah thought as she strode up the path to Todd's place. *She's living her best, healthiest life and setting herself up for success. She walks to the health food store, preps her food for the week, and hightails it to yoga! It only gets better from here.*

Sarah tried reaching into her pocket around the heavy grocery bags, but she couldn't find her keys. She set the bags down on the front step to root through her purse in search of the house key. The bulky leather bag was full of stuff: her wallet, granola bars, energy shots, the EpiPen for her Achilles heel of a peanut allergy, an old plastic SmarTrip card for the Washington Metro, a dozen receipts, a paperback romance novel, a flashlight... Then she came to a sudden realization and dropped her bag with a groan.

Sarah had put Todd's spare key on the same ring as her car key... and then decided to walk to the store for fresh air and exercise... leaving her keys *inside* of the house.

She'd remembered to lock the stupid doorknob, though.

Or... not remembered so much as just done it. She had *always* locked the door to the apartment in DC — they couldn't leave so much as a bike helmet outside without it being stolen overnight — and it had become a habit.

So much for success.

Sarah pulled her phone from her purse and used it to call Todd, but his cell phone went straight to voicemail. Great. He was probably in surgery, which meant that it could be hours before she was able to reach him. She could call Alice and ask to use *her* key... if she had Alice's phone number. Which she did not.

She let out a *pbbbbbt* of breath and tossed her phone back into her oversized, keyless purse. Then, she shot a mournful glance at the grocery bag, where the acai pouches and fruit sorbet were already sweating like crazy from her sunny walk back to Todd's place.

Did Steph have a key? Sarah dismissed that idea the moment it came into her head. Key or no, she had no intention of calling her mother for help... not until she'd had a chance to cool off. Jeff said their mom had gone *off* on him and Cee-cee, and Sarah knew that *she* was the real cause of that misdirected anger. She needed to show up to yoga with a smile and show Steph that she was A-okay. Not call her whining that she couldn't even manage a trip to the grocery store without mommy's help.

With a sigh, Sarah tried the front windows. Locked. Who locked their windows in Bluebird Bay?

Oh, right. Her. She had done that before bed last night. Another capital-city habit.

Sarah circled around the house, trying each window as she went. She had missed one; the only unlocked window was at the back of the house, leading into the cellar. It was long and narrow, but it looked big enough for an adult to squeeze through.

She pushed the window open and peered into the dark, dusty room. There was an empty work table right under the window. If she could just wriggle through, she'd be good!

Sarah knelt down and crawled through the window. She reached down towards the table, trying to give herself something to balance on, but she couldn't quite reach. Her hips were stuck in the window frame — the angled way that the window opened from the top made getting through more difficult than she'd expected — and she couldn't get any further. So much for that idea.

But when she tried to back out, Sarah found that she couldn't move that way either.

She was stuck.

Sarah tried to calm herself with a deep breath, but the way the window frame was digging into her stomach didn't make that easy. She strained to reach the wall outside to pull herself out, but the angle was all wrong. Then, she reached for the edge of the work table, thinking that maybe she could pull herself all the way in... but no matter how frantically Sarah wriggled, she could barely touch the table with the tips of her fingers. It was no use.

Now what?

She was trying very hard not to panic when she heard a deep male voice.

"Uh... Is that you, Your Honor?"

No.

Sarah's cheeks burned with instant embarrassment, and she froze.

She knew that voice, although she hadn't seen the man behind it in years. And there was only one person who had ever called her by that irritating nickname... ever since she was in sixth grade and she'd dressed up as Ruth Bader Ginsburg for Halloween.

"Hey Adam!" Her tone was breezy and carefree — which must have been some sort of bizarre defense mechanism, because she was currently wishing that Mother Earth would open its maw and swallow her whole. And Adam, too. Just for good measure. "Yep, it's me."

"So, how have you been?" he asked. She could hear the grin in his voice, which made everything worse. Her embarrassment mixed with anger, and her face burned so hot she knew she must be the color of a bad sunburn. Well, no wonder. She was basically hanging upside down.

Why couldn't it be *anyone* else? Todd's childhood best friend had teased her mercilessly for *years*, and he would definitely never let her forget this.

It wasn't a promising start to her return home.

Now she'd have to move somewhere else.

Like Montana.

Or Tibet.

"I've been great." Her reply came out with an odd squeak to it, increasing her mortification. She tried again to dislodge herself from the window — then had a sudden image of what she must look like from behind, and stopped.

"Whatcha doing?" Adam asked cheerfully.

"What does it look like I'm doing? I'm breaking and entering."

"It looks like you've got the breaking part down, but you're struggling with the whole entering thing."

"Har har," Sarah muttered. "Before you head out for your next stand up show, do you think you can help me out, maybe?"

"Sure thing." Adam sounded like a kid on Christmas. How long before this story was all over town? She could hear the bushes rustle as Adam approached and tried not to think about the fact that her butt was just hanging out the window.

"Okay," he said, "so how about you back out? I know

those hips don't quit, but neither does this steel window frame. If you turn a little sideways and unjam your hips, you should be able to back out pretty easily. If that doesn't work, let me know. I can go grab some of that avocado cooking spray you have in your grocery bag and see if that helps."

"This guy with the jokes," Sarah muttered. But she did as he suggested, and her hips came free. She was able to get out of the window when Adam put his hands on her waist and pulled, lifting some of her weight at the same time. When her feet reached the ground, he placed a protective hand on top of her head to make sure she didn't bump it on her way out.

She turned to face him, feeling like a middle-school kid again. Her hair was a mess and she knew her face must be red from hanging half upside down... not to mention humiliation.

"Thanks," she muttered, looking down as she brushed dust and cobwebs from her shirt.

"Good thing I decided to return Todd's lawn mower today," Adam said, gesturing to the shed behind the house. "You could've been stuck there for hours."

Sarah felt like that would have been a much preferable alternative. But she just muttered, "Yeah. Good thing."

"I didn't know you were still in town."

"Yeah, I'm back for good. Or at least for now." *In for a penny, in for a pound*, Sarah thought. She blurted, "Oliver and I are getting a divorce."

"Yeah, that tracks," he said in a casual tone of voice.

Sarah jerked her chin up, looking Adam full in the face for the first time. Which wasn't the best decision, because she suddenly lost her train of thought. Adam had grown up since the last time she saw him. He had the same dark hair and green eyes that had dazzled the girls in high school, but there was an added shadow of stubble now. His face wasn't as round as Sarah remembered it, and the strong lines of his jaw did something disquieting to Sarah's insides. Adam had always been a good-looking kid, but now he looked like he'd stepped out of a catalog. The kind that sold two-hundred-dollar hiking shirts. What were they talking about?

Oh. Right. His blasé reply to her divorce announcement. *Rude.*

"What's that supposed to mean?" she demanded.

Adam shrugged. "Nothing. I just didn't think that guy was a good match for you."

That guy? Adam didn't even know Oliver. Or her, for that matter.

Sarah let out her breath in a huff and let it go. Who cared what this guy thought?

"We should find you another way in before your stuff melts," Adam said.

"Oh man. My sorbet!" She ran back to the front of the house, ignoring the sound of Adam chuckling behind her.

"How long were you stuck there?" he asked when he had caught up.

"Not long," she muttered. Not that she would have admitted otherwise, regardless of how long she had hung there. Sarah put her hands on her hips and looked around. *How* was she going to get inside? "I tried all the main floor windows already, so I don't know how we would get in short of—"

She stopped short as Adam lifted the mat in front of the door and picked up a key.

"Todd has always been way too trusting," Adam said with a shake of his head as he unlocked the door. "I'm surprised the door was even locked. Do you know he keeps his keys *in* his car?"

She *did* know that. Her brother was a freak. Why hadn't she thought to look under the mat? Sarah reached for her grocery bags, but Adam picked them up and carried them inside. He went straight for the kitchen and put her sorbet into Todd's freezer. He smirked a bit at the acai, but he put those in the freezer as well.

"New year, new you?" he asked.

Sarah tried to come up with a witty reply, but it died on her lips. Curse that man for looking so good in his fitted coat and worn jeans. He was athletic in high school, but lean. Not anymore — his muscles had doubled since the last time she'd seen him. If not for his penchant for teasing her when they were young, she probably would've been like all the other girls in school and fallen in love with him. Well. That was her good luck, then.

"I'm on a health kick," she admitted, her tone weaker than she would like. Desperate for something to look at and something to do with her hands, she started to unload the rest of the groceries. What was he still doing here, anyway?

"I can see that," he said, handing her a container of broccoli sprouts. She snatched them from his hand and put them in Todd's nearly empty fridge.

"I'm turning over a new leaf." Sarah shut the fridge and turned to face him. "Healthy food, yoga... once I shed the ten pounds I put on over winter, I'm going to look and feel amazing."

Adam looked her up and down. "You already look amazing."

Sarah blushed and looked back into her grocery bag,

pulling out the pesto ingredients she had gathered that morning.

"But hey, it's how you feel that matters. I hope the broccoli sprouts and yoga do you good." Adam's phone rang then. He glanced at the screen, silenced it with a frown, and put it back in his pocket. "Well, it was good seeing you. Tell Todd the mower is in the shed, okay?"

"Sure." Sarah forced herself to meet his eyes… which felt a lot like hanging upside down from a window. "Thanks for the help."

"Anytime." Adam grinned. "I'll see you around, yeah? Have a good day… Your Honor."

He was such a pest, Sarah thought, but there was no real annoyance behind the words. Instead, as she started grating parmesan, Sarah found herself grinning.

4

FALLYN

"I know what you're trying to do, and the answer is still no." Fallyn grinned at David and shook her head.

For the past thirty minutes, he had been feeding her juicy tidbits of information alongside their miso soup and seaweed salad. He had been hired to solve Bluebird Bay's latest mystery, and for days he had been trying to entice Fallyn to join his investigation. It wasn't a murder case this time, and thank goodness for that. Even so, Fallyn was *not* interested. She had left Chicago to *escape* her old life of investigating one crime after another. It wasn't how she intended to spend her idyllic interlude in Bluebird Bay.

"The clients have offered me *double* my usual rate *and* a twenty-five thousand dollar bonus if I can figure out who's behind these robberies," David said.

"Just when I think I'm out..." Fallyn muttered.

David grinned and continued, "Some of the rich retirees who have been hit are all chipping in. Even some of their friends who haven't been robbed... yet."

"...they pull me back in," she said under her breath.

"The police have been spinning their wheels on this case for almost a year. They haven't even acknowledged that all of these robberies have the same perp."

"There's no proof that they do," Fallyn replied.

"Come on, Fal. Ten robberies in one year, all in the same neighborhood? No broken windows, straight past the dogs... and every time, they go right for the safes."

"I came here for sushi," she said, feigning disinterest, "not intrigue."

"All right, all right." David leaned forward and grabbed another piece of their volcano roll as Fallyn adorned a piece of salmon sashimi with wasabi and ginger.

Their new favorite sushi spot was half an hour south of Bluebird Bay and well worth the drive. The food was phenomenal, and there were dozens of sushi rolls and other delicacies to choose from. This was their third visit this week. Amazing restaurants were the only thing that Fallyn truly missed about living in a big city, and she was slowly discovering enough gems in and around Bluebird Bay to even the score. Even the diner that she walked to from the Seal Pup Inn once or twice a day had good meals and even better pie. Fallyn found herself in no great rush to leave her cozy rented room at the inn. The kind owner had offered her a steep discount, and she had paid for the next month in advance. After that...well, she wasn't sure *what* was next for her.

In the weeks since she and David Shaw blew the Emily Addison case wide open, he kept talking about what a great team they were and how much he appreciated her help. She suspected that he was trying to convince Fallyn to go into business with him. She was flattered, but not sold on the idea.

True, she found the work to be super satisfying... but she was still burned out from her years as an investigative journalist in Chicago. She also wasn't sure that she wanted her time with Shaw to turn into a daily grind of tiresome work. He might be using this new case to try and sell her on the idea, but she knew that the bulk of his business wasn't exactly thriller material. She wasn't ready to commit to a life of photographing cheating exes and chasing down rich teenagers who had taken off to an Airbnb for the weekend.

"You don't even want to *see* the evidence that Detective Jenkins passed on?" David asked around a mouthful of seaweed salad.

Fallyn smiled and said lightly, "I'm much too busy now that I'm officially a bona fide treasure hunter."

David grinned. "Have you heard back from that appraiser over in Lewiston?"

"Yep, he got back to me yesterday. I'm driving over there the day after tomorrow with the coins."

They had struck gold the month before, emerging from a dive with three tarnished gold coins. To Fallyn's untrained eye, they looked just like the missing treasure she was searching for. But she needed an expert to tell her if they were from the right time period or from another ship entirely.

Fallyn and David had gone diving in the same area three more times without finding anything else — any treasure, that is; there was always some sort of beautiful sea life to enjoy in the Gulf of Maine — but she was still hopeful. Maybe an early summer storm would kick things up a little and churn up the bottom of the bay enough to reveal some buried treasure.

They were both still hungry after the sashimi platter and the volcano roll, so they ordered two more rolls and a flight of sake to accompany them. The sake was delicious, but each small sample tasted pretty much the same to Fallyn. When she said as much, David laughed in surprise. It still felt strange to her, seeing him this lively; she supposed he just took time to warm up to people. Ever since asking Fallyn to call him David instead of by his last name, as she had for the first few weeks that she had known him, he had been like a different person, warm and talkative. Just with her, though — around other people, he was the same stoic detective that she had met her first week in Bluebird Bay.

"You're kidding," he said now as he stared at her. "Wait... you're not kidding. They're so different!"

She smiled and shrugged. "Rice wine is rice wine."

"That's like saying all red wine tastes the same."

Fallyn wrinkled her nose. "Honestly?"

"Not exactly, no," he admitted with a chuckle.

Fallyn wasn't sure what to make of this new David Shaw. The way he acted towards her simultaneously warmed her heart and made her nervous. She had kept him firmly in the friend zone these past few weeks, ignoring subtle hints that he was interested in more than that. Now, as they each reached for the same glass, Fallyn felt sparks fly when her fingers brushed his. She had to admit: there was something there, and it wasn't just one sided. But despite some close calls in the past couple of weeks — and despite some very real feelings growing between them — she had kept David at arm's length.

She liked him. A lot. And she felt genuinely attracted to him, which was rare for her, but she hadn't said or done anything to indicate that she was interested in more than friendship. It would be foolish. Not to mention, shortsighted. She had no idea where she would be living next year... or next month. Getting entangled would only complicate things.

And yet... David Shaw was occupying more of her brain than any man had in a very, very long time. He was kind and intelligent and shared all of her interests; he had even gotten fully on board with her new passion for treasure hunting. And beyond all that, there was that unexplainable spark of chemistry that Fallyn so rarely shared with anyone.

Then their rolls arrived, and Fallyn was temporarily distracted from her predicament. The food was exquisite, and each bite lit up her brain in a way that drove all of her worries from her mind. Shaw had chosen a fried lobster sushi roll topped with a garlic-butter sauce, and it was utterly decadent. The roll Fallyn had ordered was bright and fresh; it had cucumber and salmon inside with paper-thin slices of lemon alternating with avocado on top.

The food disappeared quickly, and Fallyn found herself thinking back to Emily's case. It had been truly rewarding to give her mother the closure she needed. Patty Addison and Alex, the family friend who had hired David in the first place, had been so grateful.

And yet, something about the case still felt a little...itchy.

Fallyn set down her chopsticks and asked, "Do you feel like we missed something?"

David picked up a fallen piece of lobster with his chopsticks and offered it out, eyebrows raised.

"No," Fallyn laughed. She pulled herself together and said more seriously, "I mean with the Addison case."

He took a thoughtful bite of lobster and then set the chopsticks down and leaned forward, giving her his full attention. "Like what?"

She shrugged helplessly. "I still don't get how they got her out to the ocean."

The case was solved. All tied up with a bow. The whole town had turned out to honor Emily Addison, and the two people responsible for her death were behind bars. Nancy Bartholomew had clammed up, but Chaz had sung like a bird in hopes of getting a more lenient sentence. He admitted having an affair with Emily, and helping dispose of her body, and hiding her car in his old barn. According to Chaz, though, he was just involved in the cover up. Nancy had killed Emily "accidentally" by bludgeoning the seventeen year old over the head to stop her from leaving their home. Then, the couple had stolen a boat to dispose of her body.

That was the piece that didn't click, she realized now.

She didn't believe that Chaz Bartholomew had ever stolen a thing in his life. He was used to having everything handed to him on a silver platter, including the mansion he lived in up until his arrest.

"You really think they stole a boat?" she asked. Then, the room tipped slightly to the left, and Fallyn chuckled. That sake must have been stronger than she had thought, because she was buzzed. She shrugged and waved a hand, like swatting away a fly. "I'm probably just being paranoid."

Or maybe she missed the investigative side of journalism so much that her brain was itching for another mystery to solve. In any case, it was over now. She had to get it out of her head.

"Anything else I can get for you folks?" asked a waiter who had materialized at the side of their table.

"That was enough for me," David said. "Fallyn?"

"I think I'm good."

"Would either of you like some dessert? Or some warm sake?"

"No more sake," Fallyn said, laughing. "But maybe some dessert. What have you got?"

"We have vanilla mochi or green tea ice cream."

"Both?" Fallyn said, looking at David.

He grinned, and she looked back to the waiter with a smile. "Both. Please."

"Sure thing." He picked up their empty plates and walked away.

"Do you need some coffee?" David asked with a grin.

"I do not," Fallyn said primly. Then, she hiccupped and added with a laugh, "But it's a good thing you're driving. I'm glad I don't have to gulp coffee to sober up right now. It would keep me up late, and I need my sleep. Don't forget we have an early date with some buried treasure."

David pulled a face. "I'm going to be up half the night trying to crack this cat burglar case."

"Okay," Fallyn said with a laugh. A belly full of food and a generous flight of sake had her feeling infinitely more agreeable than she had an hour before. Anyway, he kept making time in his busy schedule to go diving with Fallyn and make sure she was safe; she could at least take a look at the case he was working on. "Fine. Lay it on me."

"Really?" David brightened and grabbed his laptop bag from the floor. He pulled his chair closer to hers, opened his computer, and started to get her up to speed on the new case.

Beneath the sake and garlic butter, Fallyn caught a pleasant smell that was uniquely David.

It almost made her wish that she *was* in the market for a romantic relationship.

Because funny, smart, interesting David would be right up her alley...

5

SARAH

AFTER CLERKING for a Supreme Court Justice, Sarah had thought that finding work in Bluebird Bay would be easy... and it *would* be — if she could just get her head out of her butt.

She parked in front of Todd's house and rested her head on the steering wheel of her car. That afternoon's interview played in her head, and Sarah groaned as her most cringeworthy answers sounded through her memory on repeat.

"My biggest flaw?" she'd said brightly, sounding less like a professional and more like a Malibu Barbie. "Sometimes I care *too* much. I'm kind of a workaholic, you know?"

Even as she said it, Sarah could hear how ridiculous she sounded — how insincere — but that had only made it harder to put her best foot forward. She had doubled down on the false cheer, floundered and fumbled each reply, and left the interview feeling like an abject failure.

She just didn't feel confident in herself the way she used to.

Sarah shoved the memory aside, willing it into the

farthest recesses of her mind, and climbed out of her car. At least she had her keys this time. She let herself into Todd's house and headed into the kitchen, where she went straight to the freezer. There was a carton of sorbet in front, bright and cheery. She bypassed the healthy treat and went straight for the Ben and Jerry's.

Sometimes frozen fruit puree just didn't cut it. After the past week, she was definitely batting a thousand in the humiliation department. And everyone knew that abject humiliation called for *real* ice cream.

"Whatever," Sarah muttered. She crossed the kitchen to sit at the table in the corner and opened the carton without so much as removing her interview-quality sweater — just kicked her heels off and sat down. She'd take a bath later, when she needed to hide from her brother's cheerful questions about her latest job interview. Now was the time for ice cream.

An entire pint of ice cream.

"Chunky Monkey is basically health food," she said to no one in particular as she broke the flat surface of the ice cream. "Milk, bananas, walnuts, *dark* chocolate. It's a complete meal."

Talking to herself was a new, rather worrisome habit that had picked up steam over the past few days. But then again, in Sarah's previous life, there was always someone to talk to. She was born a middle child with attentive parents and plenty of extended family right there in town. Once she was in school, she had kept constantly busy with classes and sports and study groups, lived with roommates the entire time she was in college, and moved right in with Oliver after they graduated. Staying with Todd — who was nearly always either working at the clinic or out on the town with Alice — was the closest she had ever come to living alone. Soon, she would *actually* be living alone. And she had never had so much free time in all of her life.

She needed a job. Stat.

Sarah had just eaten her first bite of ice cream when her phone went off with Todd's special ringtone: Rex Harrison as Dr. Dolittle, talk-singing about how he wanted to chat to a chimp. Todd had watched that awful movie every day for two years straight as a little boy, and Sarah had set the ringtone to tease him. It had failed miserably; Todd still remembered every word of every song, and he had taken to going through the repertoire each morning as he got ready for work. Sarah really needed to remember to switch it back to something normal…

For now, she answered the call, put it on speakerphone, and said, "What's up?"

"Glad I caught you!" Todd said. "Are you done with your interview?"

"Yup," Sarah said shortly. She was crafting the perfect spoonful of Chunky Monkey: an intricate balance of banana, walnut, and chocolate.

"Can you come over to Alice's place?" There was a panicked note to his voice that caught Sarah's attention. "We could use some help."

"What's going on?"

"I got takeout and came by with dinner for Alice and her aunt. Barnaby was on his perch in the kitchen. I went to put down the food… and when I didn't close the door behind me right away, he sailed right past me and out the door."

Sarah sighed and put the lid back on her ice cream.

"I knew I should have clipped his wings myself," Todd muttered, talking more to himself than to his sister. He sounded slightly out of breath, probably speed walking around the neighborhood in search of the missing macaw. "Aunt Louise said that she could do it, but she obviously hasn't clipped them once since she got home. I ran out and tried to catch him, but he flew right over the house and we lost sight of him. Louise is so distraught that we're starting to worry about her blood pressure — not to mention the day's almost over. God forbid a bobcat or coyote finds him before we do."

"Alright, alright, I'm coming." Sarah crossed the kitchen and put the carton of ice cream back in the freezer. "Text me the address."

"You're a lifesaver," Todd said, and he hung up.

With a last, longing look at her pint of Chunky Monkey, Sarah closed the freezer. She slipped on a pair of sneakers that she'd left sitting by the door and hurried out, still in the stupid pencil skirt that she'd worn to her interview. Oh well. She had *plenty* of boring, "professional" clothes. Todd's text came through, and she didn't even need to plug the address in to find the place — it was just down the street from the childhood home of one of her best friends from high school, and Sarah had very nearly lived there for a couple of years. Maybe she would stop by after and say hello to Lisa's mom... *I wonder if she still bakes cookies every night after dinner.* Lisa had two little kids now, so surely the cookie habit was still going strong in that family? Sarah should really pay her a visit...

A few minutes later, she parked in front of a cute little cottage. It was just the sort of place that Sarah would love to live in... and just the sort of place that was *not* in the cards. People who owned those charming old cottages rarely let go of them.

As Sarah walked up, a tiny old woman came shuffling around the side of the house calling for Barnaby. She held a plastic bag of pecans in her hands.

"Are you Sarah?" Louise's voice was strong, but tight with worry.

"Yes ma'am."

The old woman smiled at her. "You're so good to come. Alice and Todd went that way." She pointed down the street in the direction that Sarah had come from. "And then they split off, North and South. Maybe you could look down the other way? I'm staying here in case Barnaby comes home."

"Sure." Sarah turned to leave, and Louise grabbed her sleeve. "Here, take some pecans."

And so Sarah set off down the street with a handful of nuts, calling for Barnaby in the fading afternoon light. She paused at the corner of the block, wondering which way to go. She was just about to turn left, towards a big old maple tree down the street that was the tallest landmark in sight, when she heard a shrill sound coming from off to her right. There was a high, nasal voice shouting what sounded like nonsense words. That had to be the mischievous green macaw. As Sarah got closer, it actually sounded like he was in some distress. Maybe he was just lost — or maybe he was stuck. She walked until the sound grew faint, and then she doubled back.

"No no no!" the voice said. It was coming from the other side of a thick hedge.

Sarah found a spot where she could push through;

brambles pulled at her skirt, tore her stockings and her skin, and she immediately regretted her decision. But she was more than halfway through, so she pushed through the rest of the way.

"Not like that, you blockhead!" scolded a shrewish woman with a shrill voice. Her husband threw down his hedge clippers in frustration, then caught sight of Sarah and jumped. The woman spun around and said, "What in the world? What are you doing in our hedge?"

"Looking for Barnaby," Sarah said lamely.

"Who is Barnaby?"

"Louise's green macaw."

The couple just stared.

"You'll, um, tell us if you find him?" Sarah asked, already backing towards the hedge. "Okay, thanks."

"Stop!" the woman demanded. "Don't go pushing through the bushes again. Go out through the front."

"Right. Sure. Thanks." Not meeting their eyes, Sarah hurried across their expansive lawn and out onto the next street over. She walked around the block and then back to the cottage to see if Barnaby had found his way home. Just as she got there, a motorcycle pulled up. She paused in surprise as the driver pulled off his helmet — and then blanched when she saw who it was.

"Looking good, Your Honor." Adam grinned at her as he hopped off of his motorcycle. He was wearing a leather jacket today, looking like he'd stepped out of a different sort of catalog altogether.

Of course. Todd had called in the cavalry.

"Did you find him?" Louise asked as she passed by on her latest lap around the cottage.

Sarah tried for a comforting smile. "Not yet."

"Not for lack of trying, I see." Adam pulled a leafy twig from Sarah's hair, which was coming out of its bun.

"We'll keep looking," she said to Louise. The old lady walked away and Sarah turned to Adam, not quite meeting his eyes. "We should split up. Cover more ground."

"If you say so," he replied. But when Sarah set off again, he walked right next to her. "Where have you already looked?"

"Todd and Alice went off that way," she said with a vague gesture behind them. "And I went looking off to the right, there." She paused at the same corner as before, then turned left. "I thought I'd check that big maple tree next."

"Sounds good to me," Adam said.

They walked down the street to where the maple stood, just starting to fill out with new spring leaves. And sure enough, there was Barnaby... a good fifteen feet above their heads. Sarah and Adam stood silent for a moment, looking up at him.

"Now what?" Adam said.

Sarah held up the pecans she still clutched in one hand, not feeling particularly hopeful.

"Hello, Barnaby!" she called, summoning up a chipper tone. "I have a treat for you!"

The bird made a rude sound and flapped his wings.

"Auntie Louise is very worried about you," she said sternly. "Todd and Alice have been looking for you everywhere."

"Alice!" he shouted. "I made tea!"

"Won't you come home?"

Barnaby just stared down at her, turning his head almost upside down and shifting his weight from one foot to another.

"Fine." Sarah pushed up her sleeves and hauled herself up onto the lowest branch of the tree.

"Objection, Your Honor."

"Shut up, Adam." She stood on the branch and reached for the next one. Her foot slipped and suddenly Adam's hand was on her lower back, steadying her.

"Motion to dismiss?"

"Stop it." She looked down at him, then promptly lost what she had been about to say when she realized how close his head was to the hem of her skirt. Was she forever cursed to have her butt in Adam's face?

"We found him," Adam said, "and I don't think he's going anywhere. Let's just call Todd. He can get that dinosaur down from the tree."

"I can do this," Sarah said stubbornly. She had climbed more trees as a kid than she could count, and she had spent half her childhood in the veterinary office that Todd had taken over last year. She could do this.

So why did she suddenly feel so unsteady and clumsy?

It didn't help that she still held one hand in a fist, clutching the pecans Louise had given her. Today would have been a good day for pockets, but her stupid useless interview clothes didn't have any. Or that Adam was standing just below her, looking up at her butt.

She managed to climb up to where Barnaby sat... and then she just clung to the nearest branch, frozen. The macaw had long black talons and a beak like a shiv.

Now what?

Sarah slowly extended her closed fist and opened it,

offering the pecans to Barnaby. He made an ear-splitting noise, startling her into dropping the nuts. The macaw flapped his wings and Sarah turned her face away, pressing her whole body to the trunk of the tree. When she opened her eyes again, she realized that the bird was working his way down out of the tree, flapping ungracefully from one branch down to the next. Finally, he dropped to the ground and picked up one of the pecans that Sarah had dropped.

She climbed down from the tree with roughly the same degree of grace as an irritated macaw, and Adam offered her a hand as she jumped down from the lowest branch. The feeling of his strong hand in hers caused an unexpected flow of heat through her body. She chalked it up to embarrassment and dropped his hand as soon as she was safely on the ground.

Adam crouched down in front of Barnaby and held out his forearm.

Sure, Sarah thought in a huff. *It's easy to be brave when your whole arm is wrapped in leather*.

Barnaby eyed Adam for a moment, then tested the black leather with his beak. Adam held his arm steady — and a moment later, Barnaby stepped up.

"That's a good bird." There was a gentleness to Adam's tone that startled her. He stood and turned to face her, and his smile was radiant. "Come on. Let's get this guy home."

Got him, Sarah texted her brother.

Barnaby worked his way up to Adam's shoulder for the short walk home, and they were so beautiful that Sarah averted her eyes. But she found that even when she wasn't looking at them, she could see them in her mind's eye. The bird's feet were camouflaged against Adam's black leather jacket. Barnaby was so huge that when he rode on Adam's shoulder, his head was a good seven feet up in the air. He seemed to appreciate riding up at that height, because he was calm and quiet the whole way home. Sarah kept her eyes forward... but Adam's smile and his green eyes, as vibrant as the macaw's feathers, seemed to be burned into her retinas.

"You found him!" Louise shouted when they were still half a block away. She ran — well, shuffled very quickly — towards them, and Alice sprinted over to put a hand under her aunt's elbow.

"Step right up!" the bird called.

"Barnaby, you naughty boy," Louise said in a voice that was pure affection. She beamed at Adam. "Thank you so much for bringing him home."

"My pleasure," Adam said. "But it was Sarah who convinced him to come down from your neighbor's maple tree."

"Thank you. Both of you. I was so worried. Bring him on inside, won't you?"

Todd joined the group as they walked up the drive and around to Louise's kitchen door. She ushered Adam inside first, along with the bird.

"I'll come back tomorrow to clip his wings," Todd told Louise.

"Don't you dare!" she said fiercely.

Todd looked at her in shock. "But—"

"We've been working on his recall, haven't we, Alice?"

"She found a YouTube channel about these blue macaws," Alice explained with a patient smile. "Their owners take them to the park every day and let them fly."

"And that's just what we're going to do," Louise said

firmly. "We've been practicing in the backyard and he's never gone astray."

Todd stared at her, open mouthed. "He flew away today!"

"And whose fault was that?" Louise chided him gently. "You frightened him when you went running after him like that, and then he got lost."

"But—" Todd started, and she cut him off again.

"I've got it!" Louise exclaimed brightly, turning to Alice. "We'll start taking him on walks around the neighborhood, so he can find his way home if this ever happens again. You'll help me, won't you dear?"

"Of course." Alice kissed her great aunt's cheek and then went to put an arm around Todd. "I ordered him a harness and a leash," she told him quietly. "We'll be careful. And we'll keep working on his recall. There's no talking her out of it."

Louise was on the other side of her kitchen talking to Barnaby. He was back on the huge, multi-level climbing structure that Jeff had made for him.

"Give me a kiss," she said. When she kissed the top of his huge black beak, Barnaby made a noise that was a perfect imitation of the kissing sound that Louise made. "That's my sweet boy."

She turned to face the humans in the room with a smile. "You'll stay for dinner, won't you? Todd always brings us enough to feed an army — even though I tell him that I'm an old woman and I can only eat maybe a cup of rice at a time. And Alice has a hearty appetite, but she's still just a little thing. What did you bring us today, Todd? Is it Thai? It smells like Thai. Or it did. I suppose it's cold now. I'll just heat it back up. You'll all stay, won't you?"

"We'd love to stay," Adam said, beaming.

"Don't answer for me," Sarah said under her breath. "I have plans." *With Ben and Jerry.*

He looked down at her with a neutral expression and said, "The objection is overruled."

She fought back a smile. "Stop that."

Adam grinned at her. "Motion denied."

Louise was bustling around her kitchen. She smiled at Sarah and said, "You'll stay, won't you?"

"Sure," Sarah said, unable to say no to the sweet old lady. "I would love to. Thank you."

Adam's grin was victorious — and this time, Sarah couldn't help but smile back.

6

CEE-CEE

"And take one more deep breath," Steph said in the melodic, Zen voice that she used when teaching yoga. She basically slipped into an alter ego at the beginning of each class, and each time Cee-cee watched that transformation, she felt simultaneously proud and amused.

"Don't... forget... to breathe," Anna said quietly, mimicking their sister's tone. Cee-cee stifled a laugh. Anna was in child's pose on her beach towel — and had been through most of the second half of the class. She caught Cee-cee's eye and muttered, "Remind me to check the level next time before I agree to beach yoga."

"You're the baby of the family," Cee-cee teased her. "Shouldn't you be... I don't know, more spry?"

Anna snorted.

"At least we're outside," Cee-cee said. It was a glorious summer morning. The sun shone high above the ocean, melting away all of the tension in her muscles that usually kept her from easing into the more difficult poses. The sound of waves crashing against the sand helped to drown out the thoughts that had been plaguing Cee-cee all week.

She had been a ball of stress for days. Between the usual business of running her cupcake shop, a potential snafu with one of the satellite location franchise sales, and her suspicions about Nate's involvement in Emily Addison's disappearance? Well, it was a lot. Cee-cee tried to follow the class into Half Moon Pose and toppled face first onto her towel. Her fall from grace sent Anna into a fit of giggles, which earned them both an exasperated look from Steph. Cee-cee struggled not to laugh as she grabbed her foam brick and rose up into a modified version of the pose.

"Inhale through your nose," Steph continued slowly, turning away from her sisters to offer gentle guidance to a woman in the front row, "and exhale through your nose."

Cee-cee held still in her modified Half Moon, focusing on her breathing. Yoga had been a good idea, she decided. She just needed to unwind. Get out of her head and into her body.

But as much as she tried to focus only on the poses and on her own steady breathing, to be present with the feeling of sun on her skin and the cries of the gulls, her thoughts continued to intrude on her hard-won peace.

It had been a week since she'd told Mick about her suspicions, and she hadn't breathed a word of them to anyone else — not even her sisters. She was still trying to convince herself that her suspicions were unfounded... because it broke her heart to think of the impact they would have upon her children if they weren't. Gabe and Max were grown adults with lives of their own, but that didn't mean that learning the truth about their father wouldn't be deeply traumatic.

If it even *was* the truth. Cee-cee hoped fervently that she was wrong. But still her suspicions pulled at her attention, as irksome as a bad rash.

"Make sure you're absolutely certain before doing anything directly," Mick had told her in his calm, quiet way. He had listened silently when she told him about the connections she had drawn between Emily's death and Nate's connection to her murderers. Her recollections were sketchy at best, and the Bartholomews hadn't mentioned Nate at all, but the timeline couldn't be ignored.

Why had Chaz showed up out of the blue the night Emily disappeared?

It was possible that Cee-cee's suspicions were correct *and* that the father of her children was innocent of any wrongdoing. Maybe the Bartholomews had sought his help and he had refused them.

But if that was true, why had he disappeared for hours that same night?

"*Maybe* you should let the police do their job," Mick had said in a soft, grave voice. It had been a subtle reminder that meeting with Fallyn and Shaw behind Ethan's back could've gotten the reporter and the private investigator killed. From what they had heard of that night at the Bartholomew property, it had been a very close call.

And then there was the fact that their meddling had made some waves in Steph's relationship. Ethan had been so angry at her for not telling him about the meeting and the lead that Cee-cee had given the amateur detectives, that he had frozen her out for a week. They hadn't spoken for days, not counting his one-word replies to her text messages and his insistence that he needed time to get past it. They had reconciled, but given the negatives that had come from their meddling — and despite Mick's assurance that he would stand behind her whatever she decided — Cee-cee was loath to get involved again. Why stir up trouble if there was none?

Then again, her involvement *had* been integral in bringing Emily's killers to justice, so...

Cee-cee let out a frustrated huff of breath and tried to catch up with the rest of the class midway through their sun salutations. She could already feel her shoulders tensing again, all hunched up around her ears.

Stop it, she scolded herself. *This is destress time, not add stress time.* She could think about all of this later.

After sun salutations, the class transitioned into *shavasana*. Anna sighed happily as she lay back on her beach towel and propped her straw hat over her eyes.

"Now *this* is my kind of yoga."

Cee-cee let out a snort of laughter, barely more than a breath, and settled into corpse pose. She let the sand support her body and felt the warmth of the sun on her skin... let her mind go blank... and jumped when Steph touched her arm.

"Class is over," her sister said, sounding amused. Cee-cee sat up and saw the rest of the students walking back towards the parking lot. "You both fell asleep."

"I wasn't sleeping," Anna said loftily, still reclining with her sun hat over her eyes. "I was meditating."

"You were snoring," Steph replied.

Cee-cee laughed and stood to shake the sand off of her towel. "I might not be good at yoga or meditation," she said as she rolled her towel up neatly, "but they sure are good for me. I feel better than I have all week."

"That's all that matters," Steph said. "Are we still on for lunch?"

"Absolutely." Cee-cee looked down at their baby sister. "Come on, Anna."

"I can't move," Anna told her. "I'm too comfortable."

"Help!" Steph teased her. "I've fallen and I can't get up!"

Anna laughed. "That's it," she growled, rolling over and pushing herself up. She flung her towel over her shoulder, sand and all, and walked down the beach. Cee-cee and Steph grabbed their stuff and jogged to catch up. When they did, Anna held her hand out for Cee-cee's bottle of iced tea and took a long drink.

"Let's swing by the bookshop on the way to lunch," Cee-cee said, "and see if Max will come with us."

"You've got it," Anna agreed.

When they walked into the bookstore, bell chiming cheerfully above the glass door, Max was busy talking to a customer. The three sisters broke off to browse the stacks, but Cee-cee watched her daughter surreptitiously from behind the crime novels. It warmed her heart to see Max in her element, talking about rare books and obscure volumes of poetry.

Anna slipped behind the coffee bar and grabbed herself a Like Rosewater for Chocolate muffin, dropping a five into the jar on the wooden counter that Mick had installed. Steph looked longingly through the glass at the muffins Cee-cee had baked that morning, and Anna grinned at her.

"Take one. What's the point of all that yoga if you can't have a treat after?"

"I have been wanting to try her new recipe," Steph admitted. She dropped another five in the jar and grabbed one of the Prodigal Summer muffins that Cee-cee had made with strawberries and blueberries in a lemony batter.

"So good," she said a moment later. "Do you want one, Cee-cee?"

"I had one for breakfast," Cee-cee replied. "I'll save my appetite for lunch. I've been craving fettuccine alfredo."

"Ooh, that sounds good," Anna said.

The bell above the door jangled again as the customer walked out, and Max hurried over to give Cee-cee a hug.

"My aunties and mom all in one place!" she said happily. "What's the occasion?"

"We're kidnapping you and taking you to lunch," Anna told her.

"No can do," Max said, hugging Anna and Steph in turn. "I'm waiting on a delivery. But I'd love to visit for a bit if you're not in too much of a hurry?"

"I could be persuaded to stay a while," Anna said, looking over towards the coffee pot. Max laughed and went around the counter to grab four mugs and pour each of them a cup.

"Do you want me to bring you something back from Monzano's?" Cee-cee asked. She worried about her daughter working such long days. The bookshop was doing well, but not well enough for Max to hire full-time help. It seemed to Cee-cee that Max was always working through lunch. But Max just smiled at her and shook her head.

"Ian's coming by with sushi in a bit. We eat a late lunch here together most days."

"That's good," Cee-cee said.

"I'm glad you approve," Max said dryly, but she was smiling.

"How's his escape room business doing?" asked Steph.

"Great!" Max said brightly. "He just added two more rooms. Technically five, since they lead into each other, but you know what I mean. Two more challenges. I helped him with the *Chronicles of Narnia* one, where the first room is modeled after, like, this English countryside bedroom in the forties. Then you go through an actual wardrobe and the next two rooms are Narnia themed, first this winter wonderland — it's *big*, he finally used the huge room that was built to be a ballroom or something — with an antique lamp post, and then the third room is a ruined castle, like in *Prince Caspian*."

Cee-cee found herself grinning from ear to ear. Seeing Max so bright and happy, hearing her talk in a tumble of excitement, was more therapeutic than any amount of beach yoga.

"That sounds like a lot of work," Steph said.

"Yeah, it was. Jeff was a huge help, but Ian did all the painting himself. I helped with the puzzles. We're going to do some cross promotions between the literary-themed rooms and the bookshop." Max took a deep breath, sipped her coffee, and continued: "But the other one, I didn't help at all. I wouldn't even let him tell me about it. I never get to really experience the rooms because I'm always helping Ian create them, so I wanted there to be just one challenge that I don't know anything about. I think he went full haunted mansion vibe with this one — he's going to do more of those as we get closer to Halloween — but I don't know the details. It's ready now, and Sarah and I are going to go through it together in a couple days. I'm so excited!"

"I love having both my nieces in town," Anna said.

"Right?" Max chirped. "I can't believe that all of us are back in Bluebird Bay. Just a few years ago we were so scattered — you globe trotting and the rest of us off to college. Getting Sarah back is the final piece of the puzzle. I hope she stays for good."

"That's the thing about growing up somewhere as magical as Bluebird Bay," Steph said. "Nowhere else ever quite measures up. I was so happy to come back home after vet school and start a practice here in Maine."

"I've been to plenty of places that are just as magical as Bluebird Bay," Anna said complacently, "but I wouldn't trade this family for the seven wonders of the world."

"Anna," Cee-cee said, suddenly teary-eyed.

"Aw, don't go all mushy on me," Anna protested.

Cee-cee laughed and dabbed at her eyes. "Fine."

"Anyway, I want to have my cake and eat it too. I still think we should do a crazy family trip this winter. Thailand or Bali or something. Beckett finally got his passport, and Nikki just sent off for hers."

"I don't know if I could leave the shop for that long," Cee-cee demurred.

"Sure you can! Slow season! Sunshine!"

Cee-cee smiled. "I'll think about it."

"Seize the day!"

"I said I'd think about it!"

Anna harrumphed and took a long sip of coffee. She looked at Steph. "Do you think Sarah will still be around this winter?"

Steph looked stricken. "I don't know. I don't think she tells me much anymore."

"Don't say that," Cee-cee told her. "This whole thing came as a shock to her, that's all. She's home now."

"Don't tell Sarah," Max said conspiratorially, "but I'm kind of glad she left Oliver in DC."

Cee-cee's eyebrows shot up. "Why?"

"She can do better, don't you think? I always thought Oliver was a bit of a wet blanket."

"Same," Anna said instantly.

"Hey!" Cee-cee said, biting back a giggle. "That poor guy."

"What?" Anna said. "It's true!"

Steph laughed unsteadily. "What was wrong with Oliver?"

Max wrinkled her nose. "What was right with Oliver?"

"He was... steady," Steph said. "Responsible."

"Boorriing," Anna intoned.

Steph chuckled and shrugged. "I'm just relieved that she didn't go through some sort of awful, gutting heartbreak like a death or an affair."

Cee-cee's stomach dropped a notch, and she took a sip of her coffee. Max looked away, suddenly quiet, and Steph's face blanched.

"Oh my god!" she exclaimed, looking from Max to Cee-cee. "I didn't mean like your... like you and Nate. Max, honey, I am so sorry. I wasn't meaning to throw stones at your dad. I just meant in general, it's an amicable split."

Max forced a smile and waved away Steph's apologies. "It's fine, Aunt Steph. I know my dad's strengths and his faults. I've come to terms with who he is... and who he isn't. It's fine."

Cee-cee looked thoughtfully at her daughter, utterly unconvinced. She sat with the fear of how it would affect

Max if she found out that her father was even less of a decent human being than he seemed to be.

At the same time, she felt a sudden chill at the now-too-familiar thought: What if someone had stolen Max from her in the way that Emily had been taken from Patty? Her life snuffed out before she'd even had the chance to grow into herself?

She felt steadier, suddenly, as all of the anxious deliberations of the past week fell away. She knew now — had always known, though she had tried to convince herself otherwise — that she couldn't just bury this under the rug. She had to know the truth.

Cee-cee would proceed with a *ton* of caution, but she would keep going until she felt one hundred percent confident that Nate had zero involvement with Emily's disappearance... or until she had evidence that proved otherwise.

Step one would be to see the man face to face again soon, and see if he seemed better... or at least less weird. They weren't married anymore, but they had been for thirty long years. She knew him better than anyone else. She'd smelled a rat when he was in deep debt, and she'd brought about a solution before anything could happen to traumatize her kids. She knew him. And if he was hiding something, she would be able to tell.

7

FALLYN

"I TOLD you we should have gone with that private detective in Bangor," Jean Keller told her husband before David and Fallyn were even out the door. "These people have no idea what they're doing."

"Thanks so much for your time!" Fallyn said from the doorway, her voice viciously bright. "You have a great day now!"

"I will *not* have a great day until my jewels are returned to me," Jean snapped. "You have no idea what those pieces mean to me. How hard my husband worked to pay for those one of a kind works of art. Because that's what they were. What they are. They're art."

The woman seemed close to indignant tears. Fallyn looked to David for backup, but he was already waiting out by the car. When Jean spoke again, though, there was no trace of tears in her voice; her tone was harsh and sharp.

"I expect results *yesterday*, do you hear me?"

"Sure thing," Fallyn said with a sage nod. "Yesterday. Talk to you then."

She sprinted to the car and all but dove into the passenger seat. David smiled at her as she drew the seatbelt across her chest, and she glowered at him.

"I hate you."

"Every man for himself in those types of situations. We need to work on your getaway skills," David said sardonically. "Why do you always linger?"

Fallyn sighed and looked out at the wildflowers that colored the roadside. He did have a point...

"Great question. In case they say something worth hearing, I guess? Old habits of a past life."

Or maybe she was weirdly vulnerable to wealthy, bitter women. There was some element of childhood trauma there, but she had no inclination to dig deeper into it than that. Instead, she said, "Back when I was interviewing dozens of people a week as a reporter, I learned to wait them out. Usually the best information would come at the end, after I'd turned off whatever recording device I was using or put away my pen and paper. Right before I was ready to go, they'd let slip some little detail that was the key to everything."

"And did Jean Keller let slip some vital clue?" David asked, eyes on the curving road that had taken them up to the Keller's manor house.

"Nope."

The truth was, their third interview of the day had been as fruitless as the first two. They had spent their entire morning in "The Berries" as the locals liked to refer to their rich little neighborhood in Ellsworth, a town neighboring Bluebird Bay. And each stop had been worse than the one before it.

The woman on Elderberry Lane had been outwardly

polite, but so arrogant that Fallyn had felt like clubbing her over the head with her own abstract sculptures. She had name-dropped ten celebrities in the first five minutes, but gave them absolutely no information that might help them catch the cat burglar who had been preying on the neighborhood for months. A grumpy old man on Boysenberry Circle had told Fallyn that she would be prettier if she smiled more.

And the Kellers of Huckleberry Court had been even more insufferable — Jean in particular.

Fallyn could understand the woman's anger... but it was so bizarre that these people cared more about missing jewels than then did about people being in their *homes*. Their safe spaces. Then again, she supposed that people who were this wealthy were accustomed to having relative strangers in their homes. The houses were always busy with nannies, maids, cooks, gardeners... people that the owners seemed to regard as part of the backdrop of their lives, hardly worth mentioning. The Kellers even had a *butler*. Fallyn found herself wondering if the man's English accent was real or if he had put it on to get a high-paying job.

They arrived at a massive iron gate barring their entrance to the next mansion of the day. It was the largest that they had seen yet: a huge, relatively modern house of wood and windows that looked more like a ski lodge than a private residence.

David pressed a button at the gate, and a man answered. "Hello?"

"Hi, is this Charles Ericson? This is David Shaw."

There was a buzzing noise, and the gate swung slowly open.

"Come on in, Dave," said the voice through the speaker.

David parked at the top of a driveway that was basically its own street, and they climbed a flight of steps up to the front door. Fallyn rang the bell, and it was a long while before they heard the answering footsteps. And no wonder. It must take five minutes just to walk from one end of this house to the other.

The man who answered the door was so huge that Fallyn's first thought was to wonder if he was a retired football player — or at least the son of one. He was only slightly taller than David, but he was a massive wall of a man.

"Charles?" David asked, betraying no shock at the man's size.

"That's me," he said in an easy voice. "Come on in."

Three Doberman Pinschers rushed up to them when they stepped inside. They seemed friendly enough. All three of them were muscular dogs with cropped ears and tails, their coats a deep chestnut brown instead of the more common black. They sniffed at Fallyn and David before turning to trot after their master. The wood-paneled foyer was a ridiculous size, even for a man like Charles, but he moved through it with an easy, familiar sort of comfort. He wore a silk Hawaiian shirt in a subtle pattern of subdued colors. His pants were definitely tailor made, and his shoes looked like they cost more than the fishing boat that took Fallyn and David out diving.

"Svetlana made tea." Charles gestured to the refreshments set out on a wide coffee table and invited them to sit as he sank into a leather couch the size of David's car. "You wouldn't believe how many housekeepers I had to go through before I found one that could make a decent pitcher of sweet tea. My mama was from the south — an exemplary housekeeper, mind — and I know what tea should taste like. But these foreign women, you'd think it was rocket science."

Fallyn stared at him, transfixed by the way he said such hateful things in a tone of easy good humor.

"And the locals are even worse," Charles continued. "Most of them have no work ethic at all. I'd come around the corner and find them just sitting there on their phone. On the clock. I fired the last local girl after things went missing the first time. I rethought that after the second robbery, of course, but I just couldn't see the sense in hiring back someone who hardly worked to begin with. I was lucky to find Svetlana. That woman runs a tight ship, and she keeps the other maids in line. Try the tea, please. Best you'll find in Maine."

Charles leaned forward to pour the ice tea into three tall glasses.

"Thank you," David said after taking a long drink. "That's delicious."

"Told you," Charles said with a self-satisfied smile.

"Now, I'd appreciate it if you would tell us everything you can remember about the robberies."

Charles nodded. "I don't know if they were different people — I can't imagine that two different people got past my alarm system in such a short time — but the robberies themselves sure were different. The first time, the window was wide open and they went straight for the safes. The second time, they actually *broke* a window and the room the burglar got into had been trashed. Took my best whisky, a six-figure single malt older than your lady friend here."

Did the man seriously mean that he had paid over one

hundred thousand dollars for a bottle of booze? Fallyn set aside the nonsense of the whiskey and the man's rudeness in favor of what was, in her mind, the most pressing question: "If you think the robber got in through an open window, why did you fire the maid?"

Charles shot her a patronizing smile and shook his head. "Well, they're supposed to lock the windows after they wash them, aren't they?" He rolled his eyes and looked back at David before continuing. "The first time, though, he went right for the safes. I have four in the house, and he found and cracked every single one. Left the guns, but took everything of value. Even the stuff that would be of no value to anyone but me. Paperwork and such...Maybe he was just in a hurry to empty them, but it really caused me a whole lot of grief."

David was taking notes. "And this happened when you were out of town?"

"Yep. I was gone for a week. I'm not sure exactly when it happened, within those dates I already gave the police. The man must have disarmed the alarm system and then reactivated it when he left. Stroke of genius, that. I get updates on my phone when it's not set by a certain time. I get updates when it's disarmed too, come to that, but I had the neighbor kid coming and going a few times a day, taking care of my dogs." Charles smiled and reached out to pet the closest Doberman. "I breed them, you know. Just for the fun of it. They go for about three grand each, though. AKC champions, these guys. Look at those coats. Gaston, here, gets a dozen raw egg yolks every day, don't you boy?"

Gaston wagged his stump of a tail.

"Pardon me," Charles said as he pulled a vibrating cell phone from his pocket. "That's my assistant calling." He answered the phone with a brisk greeting, listened for a moment, and hung up without saying goodbye.

"I'm afraid that's all the time I have for today," Charles told them, rising to his feet. "I have a business associate holding on my office line, and I would prefer not to keep him waiting. I'll have my assistant email you the details of my security systems and each of my safes — the old ones, that is," he added with a grin. "I've had them all replaced now, but I know any detail can help. I've wondered myself if the thief is connected to the company that *installs* the security systems. You two should check on that."

For just a moment, he reminded Fallyn of a young boy on the trail of a mystery. It was an absurd thought, given his size, and she bit back a grin.

"Thank you for your time," David said, offering Charles his hand.

"Of course. Thank you, Dave. I'm confident you can get the job done. We've certainly made it worth it for you." He let out a low rumble of a laugh, then gestured to an older woman who had appeared behind them. "Svetlana will show you out. Good luck to you, Dave."

Charles turned and walked away, Dobermans following close behind.

"It's weird how far a cheerful attitude can go towards making an asinine human being tolerable," Fallyn muttered when they were safely back in the car.

"You were unusually quiet," David observed as he drove away from the mansion.

"He didn't need much encouragement," she said with a shrug. "And I was worn out from the first three interviews."

"Well, that's it for today. How about stopping for a late lunch on the way back to the office?"

"Sounds good," Fallyn agreed. It would be a bit of a drive, either way. Most of these people lived far enough away from anyone else to give themselves the illusion of being masters of their own domain — though they did have some interviews coming up with people down on Blueberry Street who lived within shouting distance of their neighbors.

"The burglar obviously doesn't care about dogs or alarm systems," David mused. "One of the people we're interviewing tomorrow was even home when the robbery happened, asleep in her bed. These extra patrols might help, but the cops are spread pretty thin. They can't watch every mansion every night. I hear a couple of the victims' friends have hired their own private security."

Fallyn made a noncommittal sound. After meeting five of the so-called victims today, she wasn't feeling particularly sympathetic. But she had to admit, the twenty-five thousand-dollar reward hanging over their heads was a particularly tasty-looking carrot.

Her phone rang then, and her heart jumped with excitement.

"It's the appraiser," she told David as she picked up. "Hello? Did you get an ID on the coins?"

"Hey there, Fallyn. Not yet, sorry. Turns out, the place I sent them to, the real expert doesn't even work there anymore. The young folks they've got left are no better than me, couldn't give me an accurate date on them, worn as they are."

"Oh," Fallyn murmured, deflating.

"Don't lose hope just yet, kid. I've got one more lady I can ask. And if *she* won't look at them, there are a couple old goats I might be able to nudge out of retirement for an hour. Okay if I keep your coins just a bit longer?"

"Sure," she told him. "That's fine. Thank you."

"My pleasure. I'll call you as soon as I've got an answer for you."

"Okay. Thanks again."

"Not as old as you'd hoped?" David asked gently.

"He doesn't know. No answer yet."

"So there's still a chance," he said in an unusually bright tone. "Keep your chin up!"

His antics worked — that chipper tone from the usually reserved David Shaw was enough to make Fallyn smile. David shot her a grin and looked back at the road.

"Anyway," he said, "don't forget that we have a dive scheduled in three days. We'll keep looking, yeah? Fortune hunting is a marathon, not a race."

She shot him a raised brow. "Technically, a marathon *is* a race..."

"A sprint then, smart alec."

"Takes one to know one," Fallyn muttered, but her good humor was back. She felt hopeful about the dive, and hopeful that she might get the answer she was looking for about the coins after all. They were cool pieces, whenever they were from. And diving itself was magic enough. Especially with a buddy.

Shaw had been good to her. He deserved a slightly less grumpy partner.

Fallyn twisted around in her seat to grab a thick stack of folders from the back. It had long lists of all of the high-dollar homes in the area, both the ones that had been robbed in the past year and the ones that hadn't...yet. She flipped through them as Shaw drove, trying to find some sort of rhyme or reason to it all.

Why some homes over others? At first, she'd thought it was just about opportunity... but there were huge homes with junk security systems that had gone untouched. Even homes that had been left empty all winter... their owners had come back to find everything safe and secure.

Meanwhile, one of the houses that was robbed first had a pair of pit bulls and a security system sticker on the door. Not an actual security system, mind... but plenty of other houses had those, and the thief had gone through them like a fish through water.

None of it made any sense.

Unless...

She shot up straight in her seat. "What if the targets aren't random?" she asked, looking over at David. "What if the victims of the theft are somehow connected?"

8

SARAH

Two days after her run-in with Adam and Barnaby, Sarah had another job interview. There was an associate position available at a small, female-owned law firm in Bluebird Bay. It was located in the Myer's Building, and the cafeteria alone would have been enticement enough for Sarah to apply for a job there. But the women she met with today were everything that she inspired to be: intelligent, successful, warm, and professional. She had managed not to fumble this one, and she was feeling hopeful about it... but sitting and waiting by the phone the same day as her interview would have been pointless. Anyway, she had a fun day planned with her family. Ian had invited them to test his newest escape room, and they'd all go out for drinks afterwards.

Sarah parked in front of the massive Victorian mansion that Max's boyfriend had purchased and converted into an escape room business. From what Max had told her, Ian had only used about half of the available space so far. He was expanding slowly, as his business grew, and the room they were testing today was the first in a series of spooky rooms that would be up and running for Halloween. It wasn't the sort of thing that Sarah usually went in for, but with Ian at the helm and her brothers by her side, it seemed harmless enough. Anyway, she had always enjoyed puzzles and logic problems. It would be a fun diversion.

Surely, the women who had interviewed her today wouldn't be making any decisions tonight... but Sarah couldn't resist checking her phone one last time. There were no missed calls or text messages, and no new emails except for a handful of library notifications telling her that the books she'd ordered were ready for pick up. She turned her phone off and put it in her glove compartment so she wouldn't be tempted to check it. Max had told her that there were no phones allowed in the escape rooms anyhow.

As she stepped out of her car, Sarah heard the telltale roar of a motorcycle... no way. She turned, full of butterflies and dread, to see Adam pulling up to the curb. Todd pulled up behind him in his Jeep, and Sarah felt an irrational flash of anger towards her big brother. Todd had *not* mentioned that he'd invited Adam. But then again, Sarah hadn't given him any indication that he shouldn't invite his friend, or that he should warn her if he did. After all, what was she supposed to say?

Hey Todd, I'm uncomfortably attracted to and simultaneously annoyed by your best friend, so can you, like... not invite him places? Yeah? Thanks, glad we had this talk.

She fixed a smile on her face as Adam took off his helmet and grinned at her. "You're looking pretty tonight, Your Honor."

"Thanks," Sarah muttered. Her cheeks burned as she glanced down at her fitted jeans and silk blouse. She'd been enamored with the rich crimson color when she'd seen it in the local boutique the other day, and it did seem to suit her... but now she wondered if she wasn't overdressed for escape rooming.

She looked back up at Adam, who was mouthwateringly gorgeous in his t-shirt and faded jeans... and quickly pulled her gaze away, looking over at Jeff and Alice as they hopped out of Todd's Jeep. Alice ran up to hug Sarah, then turned to Adam with a sunshine smile.

"Thanks again for rescuing Barnaby," she told them. "Auntie Louise thinks Adam is a real-life action hero. She keeps referring to him as her Angel in Leather."

Adam shot Sarah a grin. She just rolled her eyes and trotted up the stairs after Jeff... but she could *feel* Adam's eyes on her as he followed, and her cheeks were burning again. Her face must be nearly the same color as her shirt. So much for a relaxing evening with family.

"Welcome to the Whaley House," Ian greeted them in his spookiest voice. He walked backwards, leading them up the stairs as he intoned, "Your cousin, Violet Whaley, is the last surviving member of her immediate family. The others perished tragically, all within the space of a year. Violet returned home three days ago to collect her things before the bank sold her family home... but no one has seen her since. Neighbors tell you that they've heard Joseph Whaley shouting and his wife Minerva wailing, mourning her lost children. They've heard a baby crying and the sound of a piano being played, the same sound over and over... they've even said they've heard the voice of Violet's older sister, Prudence... but Prudence was taken to the sanatorium two years ago, and there she perished. Or so Violet was told."

Ian opened a door on the second floor, and they walked into an old-fashioned parlor room, complete with an old upright piano. Its keys were yellow with age. The lantern-style lights on the walls flickered, their low yellow bulbs mimicking the light of flames.

"When you walk in," Ian continued, "the front door closes behind you, and no one can open it. What's more, you can hear a voice from deep within the house. Not Joseph or Prudence, but Violet. It's been three days, and her voice is weak with thirst and hunger. She doesn't have much time left. And without the last Whaley to lead you safely out, there's no telling what the ghosts might do."

Ian dropped out of character long enough to peck Max on the cheek and give them all a wink. Then, he stepped out of the room and shut the door behind him. A clock on the wall started counting down from sixty minutes, and Sarah's brothers sprang into action.

"There's a combination lock on this door," Jeff said, examining the door on the opposite side of the parlor. "It has six numbers."

"I found a scrap of paper," Todd said. "It looks like a piece of a letter."

They flipped through antique books — Max's contribution, no doubt — and looked under doilies in search of more pieces of the elusive letter. Sarah found a scrap of it between the cushions of the faded velvet sofa, and Alice found another in the books of music on the piano. They pieced the tattered scraps of paper together. It was a letter from Prudence Whaley to her sister Violet, begging for help. In it, she bemoaned the loss of her baby, whom her mother had passed off as her own when the family sent Prudence to the sanatorium.

"Try this date," Adam said to Jeff, who was nearest to the door. "The date the youngest Whaley child was born... one - zero - one - three - eight - seven."

"Got it!" Jeff crowed. He pulled off the lock and pushed the door open, and the others rushed through after him. But before Sarah had time to cross the room, the door swung shut all on its own. She tried the handle, but it was locked. She threw a panicked look over her shoulder at Adam, who was the only other person left in the first room – and then the lights went out.

Sarah screamed. It was pitch black now, so dark that she couldn't even see her hand in front of her face. Even the red numbers of the timer had gone dark.

"Hey, it's okay." There was a tremor to Adam's voice. Not fear, she realized immediately. Suppressed laughter. Sarah aimed a halfhearted kick into the darkness at shin level, but it didn't connect with anything. There was spooky music playing now, like a ghost had found the piano. Just five notes, over and over again. Sarah stared into the darkness, marveling at the fact that people did this for fun. Why had she let Max rope her into this? Why did it have to be the *spooky* room?

"Sarah?" Adam asked. "Are you okay?"

"I'm fine," she said shortly.

In a light tone, he said, "As often as I imagined the two of us locked in a dark room together, I could've done without the expression of doom on your face when you realized you were stuck with me. Sort of takes the fantasy out of it."

He was joking. She knew that. But she couldn't help but wonder if Adam knew that back in high school, she had secretly imagined the same thing so many times. But this wasn't Spin the Bottle or Seven Minutes in Heaven, and they weren't fourteen and sixteen anymore. She forced those embarrassing memories away and focused on the task at hand.

"Okay," she muttered, thinking out loud, "so we can't see... So I assume we have to find a light source."

Adam chuckled. "There's my valedictorian. Alright, let's feel around the walls and floor." His voice was closer now, and Sarah edged away.

"You feel that way," she said darkly. "I'll feel this way."

"Are you... pointing?" Adam asked, sounding like he might laugh again. "In the dark?"

"*No*," Sarah lied. "I just meant, you... look over there where you are. And I'll start with this wall to the left of the door."

"Yes, Your Honor," he said in a tone of mock reverence.

Sarah moved away from him, feeling her way along the wall, trying to ignore both Adam and the annoying, repetitive Halloween music playing from a hidden speaker near the piano.

"I found something," Adam said after a few minutes. "This big framed painting over here is on a hinge."

Sarah followed his voice until she bumped into him, then jerked away.

"There's one hole at that end, and another hole in the wall over here by the hinge."

"Well, go on. See what's in there."

Adam laughed. "I'm not putting my hand in there! You see what's in your hidey hole."

"It's just Ian," Sarah said, trying to convince herself as

much as Adam. "There's nothing that would hurt us. Probably just the flashlights we need."

"Okay," Adam said. "Count of three?"

"Fine."

"One," he said slowly. "Two..."

"Three!" Sarah exclaimed, reaching into the wall. Another hand grabbed hers and she squealed, pulling her hand away.

"Holy crap!" Adam exclaimed, laughing. "He got me too."

"I hate it here," Sarah said.

"It's just a jump scare. Come on, let's try again. There's got to be something in there."

Sarah felt Adam move, and she did as she said. She fumbled around — there was nothing the size of a flashlight, that was for sure — and eventually her fingers found an old-fashioned key. She sighed.

"Cheer up," Adam said. "These are our ticket out of here." He brushed past her on his way to the door, and Sarah slumped back against the wall.

"There are no key holes on that door," she told him.

"There must be," he said stubbornly. She just shook her head in the darkness. She was sure there hadn't been any locks or keyholes on that door — just the combination lock that Jeff had already opened. The keys were probably for something in the next room. As she waited for Adam to come to the same conclusion, she realized that the music had stopped. As annoying as it had been, the darkness felt even spookier in total silence. A cheer from next door broke the spell, muffled as it was. How much time did they have left?

An idea occurred to her then, and she pocketed the key.

She shuffled carefully across the room until she found the piano, then sat down on the bench and blindly fumbled her way through a few basic scales.

"You're so bored that you decided to brush up on your arpeggios?" Adam asked dryly. "Come help me find what these keys go to."

"Hush," she told him, playing another scale. How had that repetitive tune gone? Just the same five notes on repeat... It had been over a decade since her last piano lesson, and she had never been very good at playing things by ear. But this little dirge was so simple. She could figure it out. As she found the first couple of notes, Adam seemed to clue in. He stopped fumbling and moved toward her; she could feel the heat of him by her left shoulder.

"Man, I wish Alice was here," Sarah muttered. "She could have figured this out in an instant."

"Well, I'm glad you're here with me," Adam said, his voice just inches from her ear. "I have no ear for music. I would have been stuck in here forever, and dear cousin Violet would be doomed."

Sarah fumbled with the keys, a little closer each time. Finally, she tried a variation in C minor, using black keys, and the door swung open. Light washed in from the next room, and they hurried through. They were in a small bedroom, and the others had managed to open a hidden panel in the wall. They had been busy; there was another letter pieced together on the bed, and the mirror in the corner was still slightly fogged up from someone's breath, a word now illegible as the condensation faded away.

"You made it!" Max exclaimed, pulling Sarah into a hug. "We only have a few minutes left. We managed to open this hidden door to the place where Violet's locked up, but it's locked and we—" She stopped speaking when Adam held out the key he had found, then said, "There are two locks on there."

"No problemo," Sarah said, feeling considerably more cheerful now that she was out of the darkness and reunited with her family. She pulled the second key from her pocket. Alice cheered and Max squeezed her again.

"You do the honors," Max said.

Shoulder to shoulder, Adam and Sarah unlocked the padlocks on the cage door that had been hidden in the wall. Sarah pulled the heavy padlock off the door of the cage, and Adam pulled it open.

"You saved me!" a recorded voice declared, and the door to the hallway swung open.

Everyone cheered, and Max pulled Sarah to her feet for another hug.

"Wasn't that fun?" Max exclaimed.

Sarah didn't reply. She was looking over Max's shoulder, her eyes caught on Adam's. He was staring at her, the expression on his face oddly serious. Then, Jeff clapped him on the shoulder and he grinned, looking away from Sarah as Max released her.

As Sarah forced herself to look away from Adam, her gaze collided with Todd's. He was glancing between the two of them with a puzzled frown. Ian came in to congratulate them, but Sarah brushed past him — it might be a minute before she forgave him for grabbing her hand in the darkness — and walked to the door.

"Bathroom?" she asked Max.

"Downstairs, close to the front door."

"Okay, thanks. I'll meet you at the bar." Sarah turned and walked briskly down the hall.

Locked safely in the bathroom, Sarah looked at herself in the mirror. The shirt did suit her, accenting the flush of color in her cheeks. Her eyes were gleaming, and she realized that she felt more fully present, more alive than she had in a very long time.

Why was she letting Adam's flirting get to her? He'd flirt with nearly anyone — though he had the decency not to flirt with Todd's girlfriend or with Max. Just because Sarah was the only single girl around, he thought that he could tease her like she was still some love-struck fourteen year old?

Well, she wasn't. She was smart and strong, not a silly schoolgirl. He was only teasing her like that because he thought it was funny to make her blush. Well...

Two could play at that game.

9

FALLYN

Fallyn tossed a clementine orange up and down, catching it without looking at it. Her eyes were on the whorls in the ceiling paint, her mind on the puzzle of the burglaries in The Berries. Too many hours hunched over a laptop on David's couch had thrown her back out, and she was lying on the floor on her back, feet up on the offending couch as her spine settled back into some semblance of alignment.

She and David had spent the whole day posted up at opposite ends of that couch on their separate computers, scouring the internet for something that might link the people whose houses had been robbed. Aside from the loose connections that tied anyone who lived in and around a town as small as Ellsworth, their search had been fruitless. She had combed through *way* too many pictures of shirtless sexagenarians in palm-tree speckled locales, and for nothing.

She caught the clementine with a sigh and started to peel it.

"We should have just *asked* them," she told David. "Obviously they know each other somewhat. They run in the same circles, and they came together to hire you... We should just sit them all down and figure out what they have in common — and *whom*."

"We may have to," David acknowledged. "But we had to at least try to find out on our own. If there's one thing this job has taught me, it's that people lie."

"Your job is a bummer," Fallyn said through a mouthful of clementine.

He laughed. It was a low, pleasant sound. "Said the pot to the kettle."

"Hey. This pot quit her joyless job. I'm a treasure hunter now."

"The reward these people offered is treasure enough for me," said David.

"Boo," Fallyn said halfheartedly.

"I will admit that finding gold in the Gulf of Maine is more exciting," he chuckled.

"Yes," Fallyn hissed. "Drop the richies and come dive for riches."

"I'm afraid I'll have to keep doing both," David said, but his voice was warm with amusement. "For now, though, I think you need something more substantial than a clementine."

It was past nine, and the Chinese food they'd ordered for dinner had long since digested.

"Maybe I was wrong," Fallyn said from her place on the carpet while David stood to walk into the kitchen. "Maybe there is no connection. What if the burglar just bypassed some places because a neighbor happened to be there checking the mail at that time or something? I'm probably just reading too much into it..."

"No," he said over the half wall that separated the main room of his house from the kitchen. "Just because we haven't found anything yet doesn't mean you're wrong, Fal. In the short time we've known one another, I've seen how strong your intuition is. I'd put my money on your gut instinct every time. I think we should just take a little break, get a snack and something to drink, and come back to it."

"My best thinking is fueled by popcorn," she told him.

"Noted," David said with another low chuckle.

Fallyn slowly rolled away from the couch and rose to her feet, careful not to throw her back out again in the process. David was at the stove, making popcorn the old fashioned way. As she watched, he rolled up the sleeves of his dress shirt. He moved with an easy grace and confidence in the kitchen, and Fallyn was caught off guard by how incredibly sexy that was. She swallowed and looked away, ignoring those unhelpful thoughts.

David was a potential business partner. He was her diving buddy. If Fallyn was being honest with herself — and she did try to be — he was the only real friend she had in the world. She didn't want to let a passing attraction muck all of that up.

Standing with his back to Fallyn, utterly oblivious to her inner turmoil, David asked, "What about the maid Charles mentioned? Granted, she didn't have easy access to the home once she quit, but who knows if she hadn't already planned how to enter from the get go."

"You think that she worked for the other families?" Fallyn asked in surprise, pulling her attention back to the task at hand.

David turned to look at her. "It's possible. Don't most house cleaners work for a lot of different places?"

"Not if the house they clean is the size of Disneyland," Fallyn scoffed, but the wheels in her head were turning. "It's possible. It would certainly explain why the thief has been able to get past the alarm systems so easily... and the dogs. Not to mention knowing the owners' schedules. But wouldn't Charles have said something if he suspected the maid?"

"He obviously doesn't think much of women," David said wryly, "aside from his southern belle of a mother. He seemed to assume that the thief was a man."

"Did you get the name of the maid that he fired between robberies?"

"I think I have it somewhere. First things first, though." David turned back to the stove and drizzled a liberal amount of butter over the popcorn. "I'll see what I can find out about that maid tomorrow."

"I'll speak to some neighbors who weren't robbed," Fallyn offered, "under the guise of asking if they saw anything suspicious around the time of the robberies. But maybe they could give us some insight into how the people who *were* robbed are all connected. If they even are."

"Sounds good," David agreed. He carried the popcorn into the living room, inviting Fallyn to follow him. The popcorn was delicious, warm and decadent and perfectly salted.

"I didn't know you could cook," she said.

"I'm not sure this counts," he said warmly, "but I'll take it."

"It's more than I can do." She grabbed another handful.

"You're kidding."

She shrugged. "I guess I could. But I've never actually made popcorn that wasn't in a bag. My life in Chicago was a weird mix of fine dining and top ramen."

"And granola bars," he said wryly. She had admitted to subsisting almost entirely on granola bars and black coffee for long stretches of time, but she was somewhat surprised that he remembered.

"Yep," she said, nodding. "I'll be happy if I never see another granola bar. I might never leave the inn. They spoil me. I'm not sure I can live without crumpets."

"You've done it before."

"Aw, but it was half a life." Fallyn felt loopy after a wasted day of Facebook research. She yawned and then ate another bite of warm, buttery popcorn. It was nearly as delicious as fresh-baked crumpets.

David yawned and rubbed his eyes. "I think I'm done for the day," he admitted. "I can hardly see straight." Fallyn felt the same, but she was reluctant to go back to her room at the inn. She really liked spending time with him, even here in his house... in spite of her reservations.

"It's been a long day," she said neutrally. She was looking at the popcorn, but she could feel David's eyes on her.

"Do you want to stay and do what popcorn is actually made for?"

She met his eyes and said with a straight face, "Christmas tree decorations?"

"I was thinking a movie," he said, matching her mock gravity.

"Oh," she said with false casualness. "Sure. I could go for a movie."

David wiped his hands and found the remote, then

offered it to her. She flipped through the list of suggestions, looking for something that wasn't too mentally taxing.

"*What's in the Attic?*" she suggested.

"Pass," he said immediately.

"*Walking Dead?*"

"I'd rather not."

"*Beneath the Stairs?*" she tried.

David raised an eyebrow. "Are you trying to give me nightmares?"

She laughed and handed him the remote. "Fine. You choose."

He settled quickly on a Jack Black movie, some comedy that she never would have chosen, but she found herself laughing less than ten minutes in. It was cathartic to laugh so easily, sitting on a friend's couch eating popcorn. Her Chicago crowd — she hesitated to call them friends — were all about abstract art and documentaries. No wonder she had spent what little free time she had alone watching old movies. That's what she and David should watch next time. A classic.

Next time? Careful, Fallyn.

The voice in her head sounded too much like her mother. Fallyn ignored it and grabbed another handful of popcorn from their dwindling supply.

Later, when she yawned for a third time, David propped a pillow between them and gave it a pat.

"Come on," he said when she hesitated. "I promise not to read anything into it. Think of me as just another piece of furniture."

Fallyn snorted at that and rolled her eyes, but she did as he said. She rested her head on the pillow, letting herself lean into him, and he rested his arm gently on her shoulder. She felt hyper-aware of him in the way that she might have felt on a first date as a teenager, excruciatingly conscious of his every breath and movement, the warmth of him, his smell... but gradually that feeling faded into an easy comfort. Her eyes grew heavier and heavier until she drifted off.

In her dreams, she and David ran side by side through a maze of dark alleys, hot on the trail of a cat in a mask.

10

SARAH

BLUEBIRD BAY native though she was, Sarah knew nothing about the local bar scene. She had moved away for college and only come back for short visits. Summer breaks had been spent working internships or taking the extra classes she had needed to graduate on time with her double major. Old high school friends had dragged her to Benny's Place a time or two for karaoke, but mostly she had preferred to spend those trips home with her extended family.

The bar that her brothers and cousins had chosen tonight was a good one. There was something old fashioned about the long wooden bar and spacious pool hall – the building itself was pretty old – but the crowd was young. The music was mellow, bouncing back and forth through time from Bob Dylan to the Lumineers. The place was packed, but Max had reserved them a table in the back corner.

"Wasabi deviled eggs, for sure," Max said as she handed menus around. "We'll have to get two plates so there's enough for everyone. The grilled veggies are good too, and the lumpiang shanghai..."

"What's that?" Adam asked.

Max flipped over the menu he held and pointed out the appetizer. "They're like fried spring rolls. They have beef and pork inside, and they come with this garlic-soy chili sauce. One plate should be enough for the table – I think it comes with nine rolls."

"How about the Katsu Prawns?"

"Sure, let's try them."

"And truffle fries," Alice put in brightly.

When the server came by, Max ordered enough food for everyone – save Jeff, who ordered himself a bowl of ramen. They each put in their drink orders for seven-ingredient drinks with names like Yume No Matcha and Lone Wolf. Adam was next to last to order; he opted for a local lager. Sarah bypassed the cocktail menu as well and quickly scanned the wine list. When the server looked at her expectantly, she ordered a glass of the Brut Champagne Rose.

"So?" Ian asked as the server walked away. Despite being significantly taller than Sarah's brothers and looking like he modeled for a living, Max's boyfriend tended to fade to the backdrop at family gatherings. He was a quiet man and the Sullivan clan could be a boisterous bunch; her aunts tended to take center stage. But now he threaded an arm around Max's shoulders, looking at them expectantly. "What did you think of the new room?"

"It was a blast!" Jeff said.

"I want to come back and try your other rooms," Todd told him. "I can't believe it took us this long to get over there."

"I loved the riddle," said Alice with a smile.

Max nestled closer to Ian. "As much as I love helping you

with your rooms, I might have you keep more of the new ones secret from me. It's just too much fun experiencing them with no spoilers."

"Spooky enough for Halloween?" asked Ian.

"Definitely," said Alice emphatically.

Adam grinned and leaned forward. "I'm not gonna lie. When that hand grabbed me, I had to bite back a scream."

The others laughed as Todd teased his friend. "Tough biker dude, huh?"

Adam shrugged. "I have zero shame about it. That was some spooky stuff."

That was something she had always liked about him, Sarah reflected as their server came back with the first round of appetizers. Even in school, when they had watched *Old Yeller* at the end of the year, there had been tears on his face when the credits rolled. One kid had the nerve to tease him about it, and Adam had given him a small, bewildered frown.

"He had to kill his own dog, dude," he'd said, wiping tears away with the back of his hand, "I'm trying to figure out what kind of monster *wouldn't* cry over that."

It had effectively shut that kid up – not to mention making Adam even more desirable to the entire female population of their school. Apparently, nothing had changed, she noted as the attractive waitress bearing their drinks and appetizers leaned towards Adam, making sure to give him a glimpse of her cleavage as she set down their drinks. Sarah felt a flash of irritation, which immediately doubled when she felt irritated that she was irritated.

The whole thing was ridiculous and she needed to just get a grip.

"You've been quiet," Alice said as she passed Sarah the glass of champagne she had ordered. "Are you feeling okay?"

Sarah forced a smile for her brother's charming girlfriend. Alice was sitting directly beside her, and Sarah didn't want her someday sister-in-law to take her bad mood personally.

"I've got a lot on my mind, is all," Sarah said in a voice that wouldn't reach further than Alice's ears. "I'm expecting the final papers for the divorce any day now, and I had another interview today. I think I did pretty well, but I don't know if I did well enough to land it."

"I'm sure you did great," Alice said warmly. She snagged a plate before Jeff could finish the entire thing himself and pulled it within reach of Sarah's corner seat as Sarah grinned at her.

"Thanks! I wasn't feeling hungry before, but those smell amazing." She grabbed one of the fried spring rolls and dipped it in the orange chili sauce. The thin, crisp shell gave way at the first touch of her teeth, and the savory filling was comfort incarnate.

Their server came by with the rest of their food, including Jeff's bowl of ramen. It was roughly the size of his head, topped with a bisected boiled egg and a variety of vegetables. That first fried roll had restored Sarah's appetite, and she pulled the tray of grilled veggies towards her and Alice.

The first round of drinks disappeared quickly, and their server was too busy to notice.

"I'll go up to the bar," Adam offered. Sarah glanced over at the long wooden bar where the bartender was filling pint glasses. "A round of the same, or?"

Sarah grabbed the last fried spring roll while the others

rattled off their orders. When she looked up, Adam was looking at her.

"What?" she said through a mouthful of beef and pork.

Adam grinned. He seemed to be suppressing a laugh. "What do you want to drink?"

Oh.

Sarah swallowed. "Glitter and Gold," she told him. She had no idea what was in it, but she had tried a sip of Alice's and it was even better than her champagne. Equally bubbly, but with a flavor that was bright and fruity and deep and smoky, all at the same time.

"Coming right up," Adam told her. He stood up from the table and stretched – Sarah was uncomfortably aware of the thin line of skin that showed between his t-shirt and jeans when he raised his arms – then walked across the room towards the bar. She caught herself watching him, and looked away. Across the table, Max and Ian were deep in quiet conversation while Jeff was deep in his bowl of ramen.

Sarah turned back to the girl next to her.

"So what do you think of Bluebird Bay so far, Alice?" Not the most scintillating conversation, but it beat staring at Adam to see if he was flirting back with that waitress...

"I love it." Alice turned to face her, leaning back against Todd as she did. Sarah's brother smiled and wrapped an arm around her; his eyes went to some sports game on a distant screen.

"I've lived in big cities," Alice continued, "and I wouldn't want to do that again. And as much as I love really rural areas, I would miss the food and the music that you can find in metropolitan areas. Bluebird Bay is the perfect blend of everything, you know? It's held on to that small-town Maine vibe that I love so much, but it's big enough to have places like this. I have food, music, family... It's pretty perfect. Two of the people in my band have kids and the other wouldn't want to leave her aunt and uncle who raised her, so we're all content to play local gigs."

"Are you making a living playing music?" Sarah realized even as she said it that it wasn't a polite question to ask, but she was distracted. Her gaze had wandered to the bar, where Adam was waiting for their drinks and chatting to a pretty brunette. Sarah squinted and realized she recognized her. Valentina Rodolphi had graduated a year ahead of Sarah and was currently batting her eyes and generally fawning all over Adam.

She let out an irritated huff of breath and looked away. She *liked* Val. Or she had, back in high school, in any case. Smart girl with a wicked sense of humor. But for some reason, Sarah was suddenly irked by her very presence.

"I could scrape by," Alice was saying, unperturbed by Sarah's semi-nosy question, "but I've been writing a lot too. Todd works all day, and Auntie's actually pretty busy these days, what with physical therapy and bridge and other things with the ladies she met when she was recovering from her fall. Anyway, I like it. And we're saving up for a house. Todd told you that, right?"

Sarah was looking at Alice's lively dark eyes, but her attention was on what was happening way off to her right. Even from the corner of her eye, she could see Val leaning forward and tossing her hair back. The high thread of her laughter above the noise of the bar was grating, and suddenly Sarah was regretting coming out tonight at all. Belatedly, she realized that Alice was waiting for a reply.

"Yes," Sarah said, nodding and smiling a few seconds too late. "That's so exciting for you guys."

"I'm in no rush to move out of Auntie's cottage, but it's nice to have something to work towards. Having a goal always makes me feel like I'm accomplishing something, you know?"

Sarah felt like she had been punched in the gut, and for a moment she forgot about annoying Val and infuriating Adam.

"I do," she said as she realized that, for the first time since she was a kid, she didn't have any goals. Nothing concrete. No tests, no valedictorian achievement, no college admittance or degree or wedding or shiny new job. She was applying to jobs, sure, but she wasn't really excited about any of them. Or anything, really. No wonder she felt like she was drifting aimlessly along most days.

"Sarah?" Alice said gently. "Are you alright?"

"Yeah. I'm fine." Sarah met Alice's bright eyes, and she felt something inside her chest open up. Alice was sweet and friendly, but she wasn't stupid. The look that she was giving Sarah now was shrewd and curious, but she was either too polite or too much of a stranger to ask any prying questions.

"Actually," Sarah admitted with a grim smile, "I was just realizing that, for the first time in my life, I'm not working towards anything. Just a minute ago, I was in free fall, and now I'm on this cliff ledge, looking at the long climb back up." She shook her head and made another attempt at a smile. "I'm being dramatic."

"Divorce is inherently traumatic," Alice said softly, "even when it's the right decision. And moving is stressful, even when you're coming home. It's a lot. It's okay to feel, well, any which way about it all."

Sarah gave Alice a genuine smile now, though she also found herself blinking back tears. "Thank you, Alice."

"Moving here was hard," Alice said with a shrug. "I came close to giving up and going home a bunch of times, even though 'home' was my mom's tiny apartment and I had nothing there worth going back to. But Auntie needed me. And then I met Todd."

"I heard a thing or two about the situation you tackled when you got here," Sarah said. "All that work you did cleaning out your aunt's house for her sounds a heck of a lot harder than me sleeping on my brother's couch. Anyway, I have family here. And a boatload of acquaintances."

Alice smiled and shrugged. "Sometimes that's just a different kind of hard."

Sarah chuckled and wrinkled her nose. "Yeah." Alice must have wondered what Sarah was doing camped out on Todd's couch instead of staying in one of the spare rooms at their mom's house, but she hadn't pried.

"Would you mind letting me out of the booth?" Alice asked now.

"Of course." Sarah sprang up and stayed on her feet even after Alice left to find the restroom. She looked at the bar, where all of their drinks sat waiting on a tray, and at Adam, who was still smiling and chatting with Val. Forget this. She'd get the drinks herself.

Sarah walked up, intending to grab the drinks undetected and bring them back to her family, but Adam honed in on her when she was still several feet away.

"What can I do for you, Your Honor?"

Sarah rolled her eyes at him but managed a tight smile for Val. Then, she looked back at Adam with what she hoped was an innocent smile and gestured to the tray of drinks by his elbow. "Were you bringing those back, or are you planning to stay up at the bar and drink them all yourself? I just coughed and dust flew out of my mouth."

Val let out a snort-laugh. "You tell him, Sarah."

Adam grinned at her and cocked his head slightly, a speculative look coming into his eyes. Suddenly, she felt as if he could see right through her, all the way to her petulant fourteen-year-old inner child who stomped her feet each time Val batted her pretty blue eyes in his direction. Her cheeks burned under his scrutiny, and inwardly she cursed herself from walking over here in the first place.

"Objection sustained, your honor," Adam murmured after a long moment. He lifted the tray off of the sticky wooden bar and started back towards their table. "I apologize for the delay. Val, it was good seeing you," he added before loping away like he didn't have a care in the world.

"That one's a real looker," Val said, her gaze following Adam before returning to Sarah. "But forget about him, tell me about you! How are things? Been a long time."

"It has." Sarah cleared her throat. "I'm well. How about you?"

"I'm good," Val said brightly. "Working a lot, and between that and Jax, I don't have a whole lot of free time. He's two years old already, can you believe it?"

Sarah had completely forgotten that Val had a son, but she smiled when the other woman pulled out her phone and showed her a picture of a chubby toddler with a wide grin.

"Oh my gosh, he's adorable."

"Isn't he the cutest?" Val looked at her phone for a long moment. "Luckily for me, his dad and I get along so we get to share him, but the nights he sleeps there, I get a little lonely. That said, I get to take him to work with me some days, so it's all a tradeoff. Luckily, I have my mom close by and she helps out when I'm with clients and whatnot. I don't know what I'd do without her."

"Family's everything," Sarah said simply. She was so happy to have hers, especially at a time like this.

Val pocketed her phone and took a sip of her beer. "So, how about you? How's married life?"

"Over," Sarah said flatly. Val winced, and Sarah realized she had to figure out a better way to field that question.

"I'm so sorry to hear that."

"Thanks." She shrugged. "We have a few more loose ends to tie up, but then we're done."

"Breakups are tough," Val said kindly. "I hope you're past it soon."

"It's amicable, at least," Sarah added, the melancholy that she couldn't seem to fully shake lately settling over her again.

"Well, that's good, at least. Can I buy you a drink?"

"Thanks, but now that Adam brought ours back to the table, I should probably go. You're welcome to come hang out with us?" she said, feeling a little like a heel for her snarky thoughts now that Val proved to be as nice as she'd ever been.

"I'm meeting a friend shortly, so I'll hang here, but it's good to have you back in Bluebird Bay. We should really catch up sometime."

"It's good to be back, and I'd like that," Sarah said. And to her surprise, she meant it.

Sarah went back to the table and slid into the booth beside Alice to claim her Glitter and Gold. It was far and away the best cocktail she had ever tasted, and she smiled as she listened to Max and Alice's animated discussion about Ian's new literary-themed escape room.

She was so lucky. She could lose sight of that sometimes in her relentless pursuit of a goal... or in her soggy waffle of a marriage. And sure, she had been through some truly hard times – mostly the loss of her dad, which had gutted her in a way that she had yet to recover from. She probably never would, and Sarah kept the intensity of that truth at arm's length most days.

But if this was what hard times looked like for her now? An amicable divorce, a long list of family members who would happily take her in, a leisurely job search...

She was lucky as hell, even through the hard times. And she needed to do a better job of keeping sight of that instead of letting herself dwell.

Val came over a while later, all wide blue eyes and glossy brown curls. She stood talking to Adam, batting her long lashes and trailing a finger around the glass she held. Sitting across the table sipping her drink, Sarah realized in an abstract sort of way that Val was giving her a master class in flirting.

Sarah wasn't cut out for any of this stuff. She was nuts to think that she could beat Adam at his own game, and she didn't need the distraction. She would be starting a new job any day now, getting settled in a new apartment, mending fences with her mom, reconnecting with old friends...trying to outwit Adam was way too much work, and Val was welcome to him.

Sarah had only had two boyfriends in her life, and Oliver was one of them. In both cases, they had been good friends first. Common interests and intellect had been the glue of the relationships... though not a particularly strong glue, she reflected now. Both relationships had dissolved without a fight.

"How about a game of pool?" Val was saying, eyes on Adam.

To Sarah's shock, he looked straight at her. Then, back to Val – no surprise there – but the next words out of his mouth certainly were. "Actually, Val, how about a game of doubles? You pick a partner, and me and Sarah will take you on."

He looked at Sarah again, and Val followed his gaze. From the look on her face, she had forgotten that Sarah was even there. She recovered quickly, though, and gave each of them a pleasant smile.

"Sounds fun. I'll grab my friend Simon and meet you guys in back."

Sarah stared at Adam as Val threaded her way back through the crowd.

"Come on," he said brightly. "Let's claim a table."

Sarah glanced at Todd, who was giving her another of his speculative looks... and then she stood and hurried after Adam.

"The last time I played pool was in fourth grade at summer camp," Sarah said over the noise as she followed him through the crowded bar. "And I was terrible *then*. I don't foresee this going well."

Adam bent close to her ear and said, "That's because I wasn't there to teach you."

Sarah suppressed a shiver at the feeling of Adam's breath on her skin. "I'm no good at this kind of stuff."

"Pool is all about angles," said Adam. "I recall a certain freshman girl waltzing into my math class and showing the rest of us up. You were a whiz at geometry – and every other class you took, as far as I know. So just... think of it like math."

"Like math," she muttered, unconvinced. It was a bit quieter at the back of the bar, and one of the three pool tables was free.

"You remember the basics, right?" Adam handed her a pool cue.

"Ball in the hole?" she asked, raising an eyebrow. "It's not the theory I have trouble with. It's getting these sticks to do what I want."

"That should be no trouble now that you're a woman."

She frowned at him. "What?"

"You haven't played since fourth grade? You were, what, this tall?" he asked, holding a hand out in front of his chest. "Shorter than a pool cue?"

"I guess."

"You've got this." Adam bent and shot the cue ball at one of the balls that remained scattered on the table from the last game. It bounced off the green felt bumper at the side of the table and went cleanly into one of the pockets. He was right; it was all angles. "See? It's easy?"

The cue ball stopped in front of her, and she bent over the table to shoot it at a purple ball down at the other end. The white ball did an awkward little hop and rolled a few feet, stopping on its own accord a good six inches shy of the ball she had been aiming for. She shot Adam a look, and one side of his mouth quirked up in a smile.

"Try again," he said, walking around the table. He was coming for her. Sarah froze. "Not so hard, and not so low. Aim for the middle of the ball, and shoot like you're going straight through it. Nice and easy."

She tried again, but Adam was making her so nervous that the ball went way off target. He was right next to her, so close that she could feel the heat of his body, smell the lager that lingered on his breath. For a split second, she imagined the taste of it in his mouth, warm and – Sarah shook her head and stopped that thought in its tracks.

"Try not moving your body so much," he suggested.

"What?" Sarah turned to him and took a step back.

"Use your elbow like a hinge." He paused, and for a moment Sarah thought that he was going to bend over her, like a scene from a movie, moving her arm along with his. Instead, he demonstrated again. "See? Keep your shoulder steady, and just move your arm."

"I'll try," she said dubiously. Sarah took a deep breath and tried to ignore how close she was. She just moved her arm at the elbow, moving the cue like it was going right through the white ball. And this time, it worked. The purple ball hit one corner, bounced back and forth for a second, and finally toppled into the corner pocket. "I did it!"

"Good job." Adam was so close that she could feel his breath on her neck – and Sarah was so thoroughly startled that she spun around, clocking him lightly in the side of the head with her pool cue.

"Sorry!"

"Ouch," he said at the same time, but he was laughing.

"You see?" Sarah tried to relinquish the long, polished piece of wood. "I'm a danger to the public."

"But you made the shot! You're a natural. Look, here come Val and Simon. You have to play." A playful look crossed his face and he added, "I promise not to scare you again."

Damn him and his easy flirting. Sarah pulled her cue in, holding it like a soldier on guard duty.

"Ready?" Val asked brightly.

"Rack 'em," Adam replied. Simon was already on it. He was a good-looking guy around Jeff's age – and he looked at Val like he thought she'd hung the moon.

It was a close game, but Adam sunk the winning shot. Caught up in the moment, Sarah offered him a friendly high five – but instead of slapping her hand, he reached up and laced his fingers through hers. There was a sudden seriousness to his eyes, and Sarah didn't know what to make of it. She snatched her hand back and turned to Val.

"That was a good game! Thank you. I haven't played in ages."

Without even waiting for a reply, she escaped into the crowd. She needed a minute, but a glance over her shoulder told her that Adam was close behind her. Another thrill went through her body, and Sarah tamped it down. She was feeling all sorts of ways, and that wouldn't do at all. She had already screwed up one relationship. And she hadn't recovered, not yet.

She was still married! Technically. Legally. She certainly wasn't in the market for... whatever this was. Not that someone like Adam saw her as anything more than a conquest. An amusement.

She had thought that he had the decency not to go after his best friend's sister... but maybe she was imagining things. The man was a natural flirt, and he liked to ruffle her feathers. Whatever his end game, Sarah needed to get a hold of her own feelings.

"How was pool?" Todd asked as she reached their table.

"It was fun," she said, trying to keep her voice light. "But I'm going to head out."

When she turned toward the front door, she caught Adam looking, his laser-beam eyes staring straight through her.

"I've got another interview tomorrow morning, and I'm, um, exhausted anyway," she continued, suddenly compelled to make sure Adam didn't think she was leaving because of him. But as she walked out the door, she could almost hear his mocking voice following her out into the night.

"Perjury is a crime, Your Honor."

Guilty as charged.

11

CEE-CEE

Mo's Diner was packed with its usual lunch rush. Lucky for Cee-cee, Mick and Jeff had already claimed her favorite table. She slid into the booth next to Mick and gave him a peck on the cheek. "Did you order yet?"

"Just appetizers," Jeff said, watching the kitchen door. Cee-cee had a sudden flashback to her nephew at sixteen. He used to make himself three peanut butter sandwiches every day after school. He'd wash them down with half a jug of milk and immediately ask whichever parent was handy when dinner would be ready. He was in his twenties now – forever the youngest of the cousins – but it seemed that adolescent appetite hadn't quite faded. One last growth spurt, maybe. She seemed to remember Gabe putting on a final inch in height when he was already twenty-two.

It would be a major family milestone when Jeff settled into adulthood. Luckily, they had baby Grace to keep them young – not to mention the adorable tornado that was Teddy.

"They have potato skins this week," Mick said, putting an arm around her shoulders and toying with her overgrown bob. "Eva insisted on bringing us some. I ordered you a cup of coffee too."

Just as he said it, one of the younger waitresses deposited three mugs on their table without coming to a full stop.

"They're busy today," Cee-cee remarked. She wrapped her hands around the welcome cup of hot coffee. She had gotten up even earlier than usual this morning to bake cupcakes for a large corporate picnic order, and she was overdue for a lunch break. It was mornings like this that Cee-cee was extra super grateful that her commute was only two flights of stairs... but she wondered sometimes how much longer she could keep up with these early mornings. It was about time to hire someone to take the early shift. Cee-cee could sleep in just a tiny bit and still go down around sunrise to frost the day's cakes.

"Are you alright?" Mick murmured. Cee-cee realized that she had been staring off into space.

"Yeah. Just a long day."

"I didn't even hear you get up this morning." There was an apologetic note to Mick's voice. He was an early riser who got up with her in the dark more often than not. They liked to share a cup of coffee before going their separate ways for the day. "I must have been dead asleep."

"It was an early one." Cee-cee leaned into him and took a sip of coffee. "I'm glad I didn't wake you. How's the remodel going?" She pitched the question in Jeff's direction, roping him into the conversation.

Jeff blinked and pulled his eyes away from the kitchen door. "It's good. You should see this staircase, Aunt Cee-cee. It looks amazing. Did Mick show you the spindles we made for the banister?"

"I don't think so."

Jeff fiddled with his phone for a moment and then held it out for her to see. Cee-cee took it from his hand to get a better look. The wooden spindles really were extraordinary. Each one curved an elegant ninety degrees from top to bottom, as if someone had taken the long rectangles and twisted them like pieces of taffy.

"They're beautiful," she told her nephew as she handed his phone back. "Really unique and visually arresting without being over the top. They're subtle and eye-catching at the same time."

"They were Jeff's idea," Mick put in.

"But Mick's the one who actually figured out how to make the spindles," Jeff said modestly. "Once he showed me how to do it, I was able to churn them out pretty quick."

"Cee-cee," Eva exclaimed, setting a plate of cheesy potato skins down on their table. "I didn't see you come in."

Cee-cee stood to give Eva a quick hug. "No wonder. It's busy in here!"

"The new cook's nearly as good as Nikki," Eva said. "Business is booming lately. Speaking of which, I've been meaning to up our cupcake order. We could sell another twenty a day, easy."

"I'll make that many more tomorrow," Cee-cee told her, sitting down again.

"What can I get for you?" Eva asked.

"I'll have a Cobb salad, please."

"Sure thing. How about you, Mick?"

"I'll have a cheeseburger and fries."

"Same," Jeff said between bites of potato skins. They were already half gone, and Cee-cee grabbed one while she could. They were divine, with a hearty layer of fluffy baked potato under the melted cheese and cool sour cream. Each one had a generous amount of bacon and chives on top. Immediately, Cee-cee's mind went to work and how she might be able to replicate them in one of her savory muffins.

"These should be a menu staple," Cee-cee told Eva. "They're delicious."

"Agree," Eva said happily. Another table waved her down, and she shot Cee-cee a smile. "Duty calls. Sit tight and I'll bring you your salad."

Their food came quickly and disappeared even quicker than that. They were all hungry. As Mick was helping Cee-cee finish the last of her huge Cobb salad, a text message came in from Sasha. Cee-cee's sweet daughter-in-law sent her pictures of Grace nearly every day; she knew how much Cee-cee treasured them.

Sleeping beauty, the message read. Gracie was wearing a pale pink onesie that Cee-cee had given her, and her dark lashes were so long that they brushed the tops of her chubby cheeks. Cee-cee showed the boys the picture of her grandbaby, and they obliged her with indulgent smiles. Poor Mick had baby pictures shoved in his face nearly every day, but he didn't seem to mind.

As Cee-cee looked at the picture a second time, she realized that Grace was sleeping on a man's chest. And not Gabe's. Sasha's father was long gone, which meant that this could only be Gracie's Grandpa Nate. Cee-cee's stomach did an unpleasant somersault.

Aw, so cute, she texted back, heart drumming in her throat. *Gracie spending some time with grandpa?*

Yeah, he sent me this photo, Sasha replied. *I had to come into the office for a few hours and I knew you were busy today. I'm so grateful to have all of you living nearby!*

"I should go." Cee-cee pecked Mick on the cheek and stood before she could give her knee jerk decision too much thought. "I have to run a couple errands before I go back to the shop."

It was a deceptive half-truth, but Cee-cee ignored the guilt that washed over her. She didn't want to worry Mick, but she *had* to take this opportunity to check in on Nate and see if he was still acting weird.

Mick gave her a slight, quizzical frown, but he just squeezed her hand and said, "Thanks for meeting us for lunch. I think we need some blueberry pie before we head back to work."

Jeff grinned. "Bye, Aunt Cee-cee."

"Bye, Jeff. See you later, Mick."

"I'll pick up some dinner on my way home. Italian?"

"Sounds great. Thanks for lunch." Cee-cee waved at Eva on her way out.

When she pulled up in front of Sasha and Gabe's cottage, Nate's car was still parked out front. Gabe and Sasha's cars were not. Perfect. Cee-cee strode up to the door and knocked.

Nate opened the door, a now wakeful Gracie in his arms.

"Hello!" Cee-cee said with feigned surprise.

"Celia!" Nate's surprise was genuine. She broke eye contact, holding her arms out for Grace. He handed their granddaughter over, looking bewildered.

"I thought that was your car out front," Cee-cee said. "I just wanted to come over and visit Gracie on my lunch break. It's amazing how quickly they change at this age. If I go a week without seeing her it's like she's a whole different baby."

Not that she ever *had* gone a full week without seeing her granddaughter... she was just babbling, nervous to be dropping in on Nate like this. "I just had to hold the little angel for a minute before I went back to work. Where's Sasha?"

"She had to go into the office," Nate said, closing the front door behind her. There was a suspicious look to his eyes – but when he spoke, it was with wry amusement. "I *can* keep her alive for a few hours, you know. I may be out of practice, but I'm not entirely unreliable."

"I never said you were," Cee-cee said, her eyes on Gracie's face. She was half asleep in Cee-cee's arms, and for a moment, Cee-cee was so caught up in the feel of that warm weight in her arms that she nearly forgot why she had really come. "She's all tuckered out."

"I just gave her a bottle," Nate said, sounding proud of himself. "She took a nap earlier, but it only lasted about ten minutes before the UPS guy came and rang the door. We should get them one of those sleeping baby signs."

Gracie was fully asleep now, and Cee-cee set her down in the baby bouncer she had given Sasha a few months earlier. She clipped her grandbaby in and straightened.

"I'm going to whip up a quick meal for Gabe and Sasha so they don't have to make dinner when they get home from work," she announced.

"Okay," Nate said uncertainly, trailing her into the kitchen.

There was chicken in the fridge, along with a good amount of vegetables, so she filled up a pot to make chicken soup.

"Do you want to peel the carrots?" she asked, holding out the vegetable peeler.

"Sure," Nate said. She blinked at him as he got to work. Had he always been this biddable? She couldn't remember him ever helping her cook. But she couldn't remember *asking* him to, either. Cee-cee shook her head to rid it of the cobwebs of a life long gone.

"This will be a good, nourishing meal for them to come home to," Cee-cee prattled, wondering how to bring the discussion around to Emily. She started the chicken boiling and brought out a cutting board and knife for vegetables. "Cupcakes are well and good, but, well – have you seen the new Sesame Street? Even the Cookie Monster tells kids now that cookies are a sometimes food." Nate shot her a bemused glance and she blinked away tears provoked by onion fumes as she chopped. "Do you ever think about the things you want to do with Gracie? I imagine cooking with her in this kitchen, just like we're doing now. Soups and things to balance out all the baking we'll do."

"I guess I haven't thought of it," Nate said. "She's still so little. It's hard to imagine her as a real person."

She's already a real person, Cee-cee thought, but she was in Stepford mode. No use arguing with the man. Instead, she said, "I guess I shouldn't give so much thought to the future, but my mind runs away with me sometimes. I wonder if she'll be the kind of kid who prances around in a pink tutu or the kind who's into mud and frogs. Or both," she said, laughing a little. "I bet she'll be both."

Nate made a noncommittal sound, his focus on the carrots. His progress was agonizingly slow, as if he had never wielded a vegetable peeler before. Maybe he hadn't.

"You just never know how much time is allotted to you, you know?" Cee-cee pressed on. "It's such a shame about that girl, Emily."

Nate cursed under his breath. Cee-cee jumped and looked his way. He had taken a small bit of skin off of his thumb with the vegetable peeler.

"Are you alright?" she asked.

"I'm fine," he snapped. He didn't look fine. He looked like he might be sick.

"I'm sorry. Was it what I said about Emily?"

"Carrot peeler slipped, is all," Nate muttered, not meeting her eyes. The way he was nursing his finger, a person might think he had cut it to the bone. It wasn't even bleeding.

"It was hard on the whole town," Cee-cee pressed. "And of course, it was such a shock to poor Gabe when that passenger of his found the girl's body."

"It was a long time ago," Nate said, not meeting her eyes. Cee-cee frowned at him, wondering if he was referring to the months that had passed since Emily's body was found in the bay or the many years that had passed since her disappearance.

Nate's phone rang then, and a look of relief shot across his face. Already walking out of the kitchen, he muttered, "I should get that before it wakes the baby." He answered the call, voice low and indistinct in the other room. Cee-cee took the lid off of the soup pot and checked the chicken. She had a little while still before she could add the veggies. The lid clattered as she put it back on the pot, and she realized that her hand was shaking. Nate's reaction had only deepened the dread that she felt... and the certainty that he'd had *something* to do with poor Emily's demise. Nate wasn't the type of person to be emotionally affected by a news story – not even something terrible happening so close to home. There was something more going on.

"Can you stay with the baby?"

Cee-cee jumped again and silently scolded herself for her twitchiness. She turned to see Nate standing in the kitchen doorway.

"I need to get back to work, and since you're here anyway... Sasha will be back before long."

"Sure," Cee-cee said shortly, feeling a familiar irritation with his characteristic selfishness. But as that flare of annoyance passed, she felt a new concern at the expression on his face. Before she could study it any further, Nate was gone.

Still, his face stayed in her mind... and the look on his face when she said Emily's name.

He knew something. She would bet her life on it.

So... now what?

12

SARAH

THE NEXT AFTERNOON, with the house to herself and still no callback from the local job she had interviewed for the previous day, Sarah found herself doubly grateful for Todd's spacious kitchen. Stress cooking had gotten her through some hard times, but cooking in shared houses and pocket-sized kitchens was its own kind of stressful.

Here she had room to move, room to make something that she hadn't made since moving out of her parents' house: fresh pasta dough. Trying to roll anything out in her previous kitchens had always felt like more trouble than it was worth, but Todd's flat countertops gave her plenty of space. Besides, cooking something special to share with him and Alice helped her feel like less of a mooch while she was sleeping on his couch.

As much as she tried to lean into the distraction of cutting the noodles and singing along to the Taylor Swift songs she had playing at full volume, her mind kept drifting back to the night before. Adam's voice in her ear, Adam's hand in hers... Sarah tried to stop thinking about him, but she was having no luck schooling her thoughts. More than that, she couldn't escape a niggling feeling of dread. Between her unattainable high school crush toying with her and the endless mire that was her job hunt, Sarah was filled with more nervous energy than she knew what to do with. Making pasta and dancing around the kitchen like a maniac definitely helped... but even that go-to catharsis wasn't quite doing it for her.

She'd had *another* interview that morning, and she'd nailed it. A huge firm down in Portland that paid *double* what her previous job had. She was nearly certain that she'd be getting a positive callback in the next day or two... so why didn't she feel more excited? Moving home to Bluebird Bay had been nothing but a hassle – she still hadn't found a decent place to rent – so why couldn't she get psyched up to start an amazing job down in Portland? It was plenty close to home; she would be able to see her family every weekend if she wanted to. Maybe it was just the sense of impending doom that she felt, waiting for the divorce papers. Maybe once she finally signed them and turned the page on that chapter of her life, she would start to feel excited about what would come next. Living in limbo was not doing her mental health any favors.

"I can work my way up and retire at fifty-five," she told the noodles, "and then I'm free to do whatever I want. Look at Mom. Finding love again, teaching yoga. She's still young."

The noodles had nothing helpful to say.

"It's a great opportunity. So why am I hesitating so much?"

Sarah's phone chimed and she brushed the flour from her hands with a sigh. It was an unknown number, but the message started out, *Hey girl, it's Val Rodolphi.* Sarah gave her phone a puzzled frown and opened the message to read it in full.

I got your number from Todd, Val continued. *I hope that's okay. Are you at his place now? Can I swing by real quick?*

Sure, Sarah replied, though what Val wanted from her was anyone's guess. If there were no Alice, Sarah might assume that Val was coming by to pick up something she'd forgotten in Todd's room one night. But failing that, why in the world was Val dropping in?

She turned down her music enough that she would be able to hear a knock on the door, and Val pulled up just a few minutes later.

"Hi," Sarah called, opening the door as Val walked up to the house.

"Hi Sarah!" Val called. "Thanks for letting me just drop by like this. I don–" Val stopped and looked at her, amusement pulling at one corner of her mouth. "Are you baking something?"

Sarah looked down at her clothes. She was absolutely covered in flour.

"Yeah," she said, giving Val a smile that felt a bit like a grimace. "Pasta."

"You're making noodles from scratch?" Val exclaimed. "I haven't done that since before Jax was born. Man, I didn't realize 'til just now how much I missed it. Can I help?"

Sarah recovered quickly from her stunned silence.

"Um, yeah... Sure."

What else could she say?

"Thanks!" Val said as if going door to door and working for free was her *modus operandi*. "I used to help the old Italian lady who lived across the street," the other woman explained as she rolled up her sleeves and made her way toward the kitchen sink to wash her hands. "We would make lasagna from scratch, ravioli, all kinds of things."

"That's awesome," Sarah said. She went into the fridge for a bottle of white wine and poured a glass for each of them. She had successfully resisted day drinking *alone*, but surely it was okay now that she had a guest...

"I bet she loved the company," she said as Val began to roll out a fresh sheet of pasta dough.

"Yeah, I think she did. And so did I. I never had any siblings, and my parents both worked, sometimes two jobs, so it could get really lonely at home..." Val started slicing the sheet of dough into even strips, matching the size of the ones Sarah had already made. "She used to help me with my math homework. And even when I got to the point that my homework was kind of beyond her, she would always set me up with study snacks. Always had a hot meal ready when I didn't h–" Val broke off and the expression on her face stopped Sarah in her tracks. She didn't think that anybody in Bluebird Bay went without food, certainly not the kids. Then again, it could be hard to make ends meet in the off-season in a tourist town...

Val met Sarah's eye in a glancing sort of way and shrugged.

"Things could get tight close to payday, especially after my dad got sick and it was just my mom working. Mrs. Fucito lived alone, but she always seemed to have plenty. Her husband's retirement money, maybe, or life insurance. I don't really remember him. He passed away, and I got to know Mrs. Fucito real well after that."

"I never knew your family struggled," Sarah said quietly.

As she filled a pot of water to boil the pasta, she thought about how Val had been in the running for Valedictorian... and how impressive that was given everything she had been dealing with at home.

Val took a sip of her wine Sarah gave her.

"This is good, thank you."

"You're welcome."

"I had good parents," Val continued, her voice uncharacteristically subdued. "My mom is amazing with Jax. I had a good childhood. It's just that they both had to work a ton to make ends meet. Mrs. Fucito filled in the gaps when my parents couldn't be there. Like the grandma I never had. And when I was thirteen and my dad got too sick to work, and my mom was working and taking care of him and just exhausted all the time, Mrs. Fucito always made sure there was a home-cooked meal waiting for me. And plenty for my folks, too. She'd send it home with me, saying that she never learned how to cook for one and she didn't want to." Val smiled and put on a strong Italian accent. "Waste is a sin. I will never be able to eat all of this food. Take pity on an old woman. Take it away."

"She sounds like an amazing person," Sarah said. "I can't believe I never met her."

"She lived outside of Bluebird Bay."

Sarah cocked her head to one side. "But I thought she was your neighbor."

"Yeah, about that...so, I didn't exactly live in Bluebird Bay," Val admitted with a wry smile. She took another sip of her wine. "Remember my friend Stacy? Her family let us use their address on the school forms so that I could go to school here. The district I lived in didn't have honors programs or music class or any of that. A couple years later, they made it a charter school, so I was legit, but until then? I technically shouldn't have been there."

"Oh." Sarah was stunned by how much had happened without her knowledge in a high school as small as hers. So many lives, so many stories that she had been willfully ignorant of. She had always been so hyper focused on the next test, the next A. She had never even known that Val's dad was sick… or that Val had lost him before Sarah lost hers. What a brutally painful thing to have in common.

If Sarah had thought about Val when they were young, it was with jealousy. Val had always been popular with the boys, and Sarah had always been utterly clueless on that front – a lack of confidence that she had covered up by pretending lack of interest. She had told herself that she was too mature for high school boys, too smart, too busy with other things. Mostly, she'd just been too insecure.

"I guess I should get to why I'm here." Val shot her a glance and cleared her throat. "You know that I passed the bar last year?"

Sarah hadn't even known that the other woman had gone to law school. "That's awesome, Val."

Val shrugged. "I had to take some time off of school when Jaxon was born, but I finished eventually. I haven't had much experience, though, not like you." She took a deep breath and pressed forward. "I came here to tell you that I'm working on creating my own law firm. Right here in Bluebird Bay. I want to work on a sliding scale for local families, and I want to do pro bono work when I can. General practice, you know, like people used to do in small towns."

"Wow, I love that idea," Sarah said.

"Enough to go into business with me?" Val blurted.

Sarah stared at her, mouth agape. "I, uh, well–"

"Sorry, wait." Val grinned in a self-deprecating sort of way. "I got the order wrong. Let me try again."

"Okay," Sarah said uncertainly. The water was simmering now, and she started dropping the noodles in.

"Last night, when you told me that you were home for good... it felt like kismet. You're the one other person from our school who became a lawyer. And I always admired you. Your intelligence, your drive, your integrity.

"The past couple of years, I've been networking. Pulling together connections and resources for this vision I've had since before I started law school. Probably since I read *To Kill a Mockingbird* when I was ten," she said with a shaky laugh. "I found a space, secured enough investors to get started, and there are at least a couple dozen people who are already looking to hire me. More than I'll be able to keep up with, to be honest. I'm a mom, you know? I can't work seventy hours a week. I don't want to miss out on that much time with my kid."

Sarah was stunned by how much Val had already accomplished on her own. "Are you offering me a job?"

"A partnership," Val replied immediately. "Rodolphi and Ketterman."

"Wow." Sarah was too surprised to process the idea here and now. She turned her attention back to the noodles. She'd need to strain them in a minute.

"I'm sorry," Val said with an apologetic smile. "I should have worked my way up to it. I'm too blunt for my own good. I'm just... the type to just *go* for it when I want something, you know? Kind of like when I saw Adam walk into the bar yesterday," she added with a laugh.

Sarah cussed under her breath. She'd been in the process of straining the pasta when Val said Adam's name, and she ended up pouring some of the hot water over her fingers.

"Are you okay?" Val asked.

"Yeah, I'm fine." Sarah ran her fingers under cold water while Val plated the pasta and drizzled it with olive oil.

"I'm pragmatic, too," Val said wryly. "I know when to call it quits – like, when a guy only has eyes for someone else."

Sarah frowned at her. "What do you mean?"

Val ignored her to rummage through the fridge for a hunk of pecorino romano. As she grated the cheese over their pasta, she said, "Just think on it. Give me your email before I go and I'll send you a real business proposal, all the deets. Okay?"

Sarah stared at her old friend, a host of possibilities churning through her head. Much to her chagrin, the bulk of them had nothing to do with her career.

She took a deep breath and blew it out in a sigh.

"Okay."

13

FALLYN

FALLYN AND DAVID were back in The Berries for yet another interview at yet another oversized house. This one looked slightly less opulent than the others they had been in so far. It was a house that *hadn't* been robbed – they were here to ask a woman named Deirdre Eddings if she had seen anything odd leading up to the robberies at her neighbors' houses – and Fallyn wondered now if this house had gone untouched because it was a bit more modest than most homes in the area. Just a bit, but enough that a burglar might pass it over in pursuit of bigger fish.

The wind whipped Fallyn's hair across her face as they hurried from David's car to the front door of the house. There was a hurricane roaring up the coast, but it was supposed to peter out and lose most of its force before it reached Maine. Fallyn hoped that they would have time to finish all three of their interviews before the rain hit – because weather forecast aside, they seemed to be right in the path of the storm.

David's arm pressed against her shoulder as they stood in

the narrow archway that led to the front door. Fallyn could feel the heat of his skin through the thin fabric of their clothes, and the brief touch sent tingles down her arm.

They had crossed some sort of invisible line the other night, when she had fallen asleep on David's couch and woken up draped over his legs. She had just about sprinted out the door.

But honestly? Fallyn was tired of running.

They were in that awkward phase: Fallyn knew that he liked her and she was fairly certain that David knew she liked him too… but they were still tiptoeing around it. He was clearly trying to respect her boundaries, and she appreciated that. All the same, the anticipation was starting to feel like it might kill her before anything actually happened between them.

David had been interested in her from the start, but he was an eminently patient man. He had communicated just enough to make his feelings clear, and that was it. He hadn't pushed for a response or drawn away. He hadn't acted weird or concerned. So far, he had simply accepted what she was willing to give him – which up until this point had been her friendship and a bit of help with this mystery that had all but taken over his work life. And all the while, Fallyn's feelings for him had grown, slow and steady, until she could no longer pretend that she wasn't attracted to the man.

Fallyn was ready to take the next step.

Or… almost ready. As soon as they were done working on this case, she wanted to explore whatever this was between them. God forbid it didn't work out, or they didn't have the chemistry that seemed to charge the air between them… Losing his friendship would be awful, but walking away from this case might be even worse. She couldn't stand the thought of leaving without seeing this through. She had always been more of an investigator than a romantic, and an unsolved mystery was her least favorite thing in the world... with the possible exception of boiled okra.

A teenage boy opened the door and led them through to the living room. It was a large space with a massive fireplace and vaulted ceilings, yet it felt somehow comfortable. The cushy furniture invited people to kick their shoes off and relax. There were instruments scattered here and there, a half-finished puzzle on the coffee table, and an oversized bean bag chair in one corner. All of the other houses they had visited so far had felt more like museums than domiciles. This one felt like a *home*.

"Make yourselves at home," the young man – he was taller than Fallyn, but still more boy than man – told them. "I'll go get my mom."

Nice kid, Fallyn thought as she took a seat on the couch beside David. She was always pleasantly surprised when she met a good-natured teenager. She certainly hadn't been one herself.

He was back a moment later. "My mom will be right out. Can I get you anything to drink? We have ginger ale."

"I'd love some," Fallyn replied. "Thank you."

"You?" the kid asked David.

"Water?" David replied. It cracked Fallyn up sometimes, how many men communicated with each other in monosyllables.

"Sure," the kid said, and disappeared again.

David had taken a notepad out of his pocket and was flipping through it.

"No broken windows on any of the houses. No smashed door locks. It has to be an inside job."

"Or such a good outside job that we're missing something," Fallyn put in. She took a hair tie from her wrist and smoothed her wind-whipped hair into a quick topknot. "What if we go back to a couple of the houses that were robbed and take a closer look at potential entry points?"

"The cops did that," David muttered, eyes on his notes.

"Maybe *they* missed something."

He looked up at her with a wry grin. "Maybe so." He looked over her shoulder and stood. Fallyn did the same and found a woman walking toward them. She was somewhat older than Fallyn, probably in her mid-forties, and quite attractive.

"Hi there, I'm Deirdre," the woman said with an apologetic smile as she held up her cell phone. "I'm sorry to keep you waiting. Just finishing up a meeting, be there in two shakes."

She held the phone back to her lips and spoke in low tones about a client contract needing to be signed as she headed back out of the room. When she returned a moment later, she was carrying two glasses, and the cell phone was nowhere in sight.

She handed David his water and Fallyn her ginger ale with a grin.

"Please sit. I'm sorry again for keeping you waiting. I don't know what made me think taking on a huge new client at the same time as prepping for my daughter's wedding next month was a good idea, but here we are."

She had a warm laugh, and Fallyn liked her instantly. Her face was striking, with wide eyes and sharp cheekbones.

Unlike the other women in this neighborhood, Deirdre's skin wasn't plastic-smooth. There were lines around her eyes and mouth that showed exactly how quick to smile she was. Her clothes, while clearly of good quality, looked lived in and she even had a streak of white paint in her hair.

"Let me guess, Antique Alabaster?" Fallyn quipped before taking a sip of her soda.

At Deirdre's puzzled smile, she gestured to the ghostly lock.

"Oh Lord," the other woman said with a chuckle as she ran a hand through her hair. "Actually, it's called Oysters on the Half Shell, and I thought I got it all."

"You should see me when I'm painting," Fallyn replied, commiserating. "My clothes look like a Jackson Pollock original."

Deirdre snort-laughed, making Fallyn like her even more.

A sudden howling sound reverberated through the room and the windows shuddered and creaked.

"That wind is really whipping up fast, isn't it?" Deirdre said as she took a seat on the dove gray loveseat across from them. "The weatherman said it's not supposed to really hit until after dark, but it sounds like it's coming quite a bit quicker than that. I remember one that hit back in the eighties, when I was just a kid. Our table – the kind with an umbrella attached, you know? – blew right over into the neighbor's yard. I already had Carter bring all the patio furniture into the garage. All that to say, I imagine you'll want to be off the roads sooner than later. So please, let's get to it. You said you had some questions regarding the break-ins down the street...How can I help?"

David took a long drink of his water before setting it on the table and pulling a pencil from his shirt pocket.

"We've just been reaching out to the homes that haven't been affected. Did you happen to notice any strange cars in the neighborhood in the days leading up to the robberies?"

She cocked her head and frowned, deep in thought. "You know, that detective who came around last month asked the same question. He left his card and asked me to call him if I saw or remembered anything odd. But honestly, I've wracked my brain and keep coming up empty. Although, I must admit, I'm probably not the best person to ask. I lose my own car in parking lots pretty regularly. Once, I even took my cordless home phone to work with me. And just the other day I found my glasses in the fridge." She chuckled and shrugged. "My brain is always churning about a million things at once, so I'm not exactly super tuned in to my surroundings. I'd make a terrible eyewitness. Keep in mind, I'm also sort of a newbie to the area. We've only been here a few months. I wanted to rent first to make sure we liked the area and the school before we settled down for sure."

David nodded and jotted something down on his notepad.

"And?" Fallyn asked. "What do you think so far?"

"Honestly?" Deirdre wrinkled her nose and gave Fallyn a shrug. "Not my cup of tea in the best of circumstances. This house is too big for just Carter and me, and...well, there seems to be a lot of hot air in this neighborhood, if you know what I mean. The robberies just sealed the deal."

Fallyn nodded. "That would definitely be a deal breaker for a lot of people."

"Do you mind me asking...does this house have an alarm system?" David continued.

"It doesn't," Deirdre said. "I might have invested in one if we weren't moving out before the end of the year. But as it is..." She shrugged. "No violence or anything reported, so I just put my valuables in a safety deposit box for now. The things that are really precious to me – my grandmother's jewelry, things like that."

"And how about a dog?" Fallyn added, thinking back to the Dobermans down the street. "Do you guys have one?"

"No, not anymore." Deirdre shook her head sadly. "Our boxer passed away last year, and I just haven't had the heart to get another. Not yet, at least. Maybe when Carter leaves for college I'll get myself an older rescue."

"Have you left home for any length of time in the past couple months?"

She shook her head. "Just an overnight here or there to visit my parents. Why do you ask?"

David was busy writing, and Fallyn answered for him.

"We've been trying to determine if the houses that have been robbed have something in common. A level of protection, maybe, or something else that we've missed. But we're also trying to collect information about the houses that have been passed over as well, to see if we can figure out some sort of pattern. Do you know any of the people who have been robbed on a personal level?"

"Most of them, I think," Deirdre replied with a nod. "Just in passing, though. I joined the neighborhood book club when we first moved here, and we got invited to some holiday parties and things...I pulled back from all that pretty quickly, though."

"Do they have anything in common that you can think of?" Fallyn asked before taking a sip from her ginger ale.

"Besides being snooty and pretentious?" Deirdre laughed, then put a hand over her mouth. From the corner of her eye, Fallyn saw David's lips twitch towards a smile.

"Sorry, that was mean. I guess one thing..." Deirdre frowned and then nodded. "Yeah, so the people that were robbed are all deeply rooted in the community, and I'm pretty sure they've been here a long time. There are only a handful of us that are newer to the neighborhood and, off the top of my head, I don't think any of those homes have been hit so far. Aside from that, I can't think of any other connections," Deirdre said, shaking her head.

It wasn't much, but it was something to consider...

David turned to her and raised his brows.

"I think that's all we have for now?"

Fallyn shot Deirdre a smile. "I think so. But thanks so much for taking the time to speak with us, Ms. Eddings. We really appreciate it."

"Happy to help," Deirdre said as they all stood.

"We should be getting to our next appointment." David handed her his card. "Please call us if you think of anything else."

"Of course," she said, tucking the card into her pants pocket with a kind smile. "You two get wherever you're going safe. It's getting ugly out there."

Like clockwork, just as they stepped foot outside, the sky opened up and the rain started pounding down in buckets. Fallyn screamed in surprise and raced for the car, howling as the pouring rain soaked through her dress shirt. David dove into the car and had the passenger door open for her by the time she reached it.

"We might have to reschedule the other interviews," she said. "I'm drenched and it is definitely getting ugly out there."

"Ms. Eddings might not be all that astute about some things," David chuckled as he mopped at his face with a damp shirtsleeve, "but she was bang on about the weather."

As they made their way out of the fancy cul-de-sac, Fallyn couldn't help but think that Deirdre had been right about something else, too.

All the people who had been robbed *were* snooty and wholly unlikeable.

Not exactly a rock solid motive, but certainly notable.

A coincidence?

Or had the unlucky residents of The Berries condescended to the wrong person and paid a handsome price?

14

SARAH

MAINERS AREN'T FRIGHTENED off the roads easily.

It was already raining when Sarah left for the grocery store to buy some stormy staples, but if the weather report was right, she would have plenty of time to stock up on snacks and head back to Todd's. She was a good driver, and it wasn't like this was a winter storm with sleet and freezing rain. Summer storms were no big deal.

Or so she told herself as she drove back across Bluebird Bay with the rain coming down in sheets. She couldn't see even one car's length in front of her, so she was driving ten miles per hour and listening to some slightly crackly pop music on the radio. The rain somehow started to come down even *harder*, and Sarah couldn't see a thing. She swore under her breath and slowed to a crawl, wishing that she had left earlier. But her whole schedule had gotten thrown off and she was an hour behind on every single thing she had planned. She'd had yet another fitful night's sleep thinking about Val's offer... and Adam's stupid-beautiful arms. She could still feel him standing right behind her, his hands guiding her as he taught her how to play pool. And, as if the lunk toying with her emotions wasn't bad enough, Sarah's own subconscious was messing with her. When she did manage to fall asleep, Adam kept on teasing her in her dreams.

Sarah shoved Adam out of her mind – he was making *way* too many appearances there lately – and turned the radio up *all* the way. Her mind was full. She needed to find a job and a place to live. She had no space in her mind to spare for her big brother's best friend. It was past time to shut those thoughts down – especially since his presence in her dreams was already causing her to make bad decisions, like not getting home with plenty of time to spare. The storm wasn't supposed to hit until the end of the day, but she should know better than to trust the weather report on an hourly level. It was already flying sideways as she left the grocery store, and now she was basically driving underwater.

She could just barely hear the music over the rain, which was pounding on her car roof like an angry spirit. A whole horde of angry spirits, she amended as the wind picked up and drove the rain sideways, pelting the window next to her face.

She didn't start to feel truly nervous until the music cut off mid-song and was replaced by the slow drone of a flash flood warning. With zero visibility to keep an eye out for the size and depth of growing puddles, Sarah drove right into one. There was a sickening lurch as the water rose above her tires and her car nearly stopped moving. She kept her foot steady on the gas, and the car pulled and swayed against the deep water. For a moment, she thought that she was stuck. But her little car powered through, and she maneuvered out of the pool. Sarah breathed a sigh of relief, not even trying to loosen her death grip on the steering wheel.

Nearly home. It was night-dark beneath the thick clouds, and her car was making weird noises, but she was nearly back to Todd's house. Well, a few more miles.

Sarah saw another pool in the road seconds before driving straight into it. She let out another string of curse words – she couldn't even hear *herself* above the roar of the rain – and managed to pull off the road. Her car shuddered to a halt, and Sarah turned it off. She could wait out the worst of the storm here, but Sarah had a niggling worry that her car wouldn't start again. At least, not until it had the chance to dry out. Todd's Jeep might be able to make it the last few miles, though.

Sarah pulled out her phone to call her brother... and it had no bars. A groan escaped her, nothing but a vibration in her chest as the storm howled outside. She should have known not to bother with a cell phone in a storm like this.

She tried turning the key in the ignition. Nothing.

"Okay," she said out loud. The strangeness of speaking without being able to hear her own voice was oddly calming. "Bluebird Bay is not that big. Your family is. Surely someone lives close enough that you could walk to their house."

Sarah went through a mental roster. Todd's house was still a few miles away, and their childhood home was further. Ditto Max's apartment, Sasha and Gabe's place, Aunt Ceecee's shop, Aunt Anna and Beckett's house... So much for family. She added Eva from Mo's Diner to her mental map and a few other acquaintances... but they were all too far away.

Sarah let out another groan when she realized that there

was only *one* house within reasonable walking distance from where her car was stranded.

And that house belonged to Adam Tedeski.

"Why are you doing this to me?" she roared at the sky, so loud that she could almost hear herself above the rain. Fickle Fate was *continually* messing with her and shoving her in Adam's path. She didn't enjoy feeling like Fate's plaything.

But there was nothing to it. She didn't want to spend the night in her car. Maybe once she got to Adam's house she could get word to Todd – at least to tell him that she was safe, so he wouldn't spend the night worrying.

The rain subsided from a deluge to simply pouring, and Sarah seized that dubious window. She shoved her paper grocery bag under her shirt, yelping when the cold from the ice cream bit at her skin, and opened the door to the howling wind. It was a slow, soaking-wet trek to Adam's house about half a mile down the road. When she finally found it, she huddled next to the front door and knocked.

No answer. Of course. He was probably shacked up with someone else for the night. Wouldn't that be just her luck. She wondered for a moment if Adam had a key hidden somewhere like Todd did... but before trying such desperate measures, she leaned heavily on the doorbell.

Adam answered a minute later.

Shirtless.

Sarah stared. She should have stayed in the car.

"Geez, woman," Adam said. "Get inside. What the hell are you doing out in this?" He was wearing gym shorts, with headphones dangling from one ear and beads of sweat on his chest. Sarah pulled her gaze away and stepped inside just enough for Adam to close the door behind her.

"Thought it seemed like a nice time to go for a stroll." Sarah's sarcasm might have had more bite to it if she hadn't had to push it out past chattering teeth.

"You're freezing," Adam murmured. "I'll be right back."

Sarah was soaked to the bone, and her ice cream baby wasn't helping. The paper bag ripped as she pulled the groceries out from under her shirt, and Adam gave her a bemused look as he trotted back her way and traded her a towel for the disintegrating grocery bag.

"Seriously, what happened?" he asked.

Sarah towel-dried her hair, deliberately hiding her face in the process. When she came out of hiding a moment later, she had to bite back a smile at the sight of a shirtless Adam clutching a pile of snack foods to his chest and watching her with concern.

"I cut things too close on my grocery run," she admitted. She was still cold, but at least her teeth had stopped chattering. It was warm inside Adam's house. "I hit a couple of puddles on my way back, and my car gave up the ghost about half a mile down the road."

"Holy crap. Okay. I'm glad you made it to my door. Let's call Todd and tell him you're here and okay."

"I tried, but there's no service." Sarah pulled out her cell phone and looked again – still no bars. "Do you have a landline?"

"Yeah, I do, actually." Adam disappeared through a doorway. He came back without the groceries and handed her a cordless phone.

"Thanks." She had to go into the contacts on her phone to find Todd's number, which she punched into the phone. "He probably doesn't have service, either," she said under her breath as she listened to the phone ring.

"Hello?" Todd answered.

"Hey Todd, it's me."

"Sarah?" he said through heavy static. "Is that you? You're at Adam's house?"

"Yeah, my car broke down a half mile away."

"You what?"

"I drove into a puddle on the way back from the grocery store and had to hoof it to the nearest house."

"Sarah? Are you still there?"

"I'm safe!" she said, almost yelling. "I'll come home when I can."

"Okay, got it. Sorry I–" the rest of the sentence was lost to static, and then she heard, "one bar – when I can."

Sarah disconnected and stared at the phone for a second. Now what?

"Here." Adam was in front of her, holding out a pile of clothes.

"What's this?" The clothes clearly belonged to Adam. Were they for her? Well, she supposed it was better than Adam handing her a pile of women's clothes. Still, the thought of wearing his things was uncomfortably intimate.

"Dry clothes." Something in her expression made him grin, and he plucked the house phone from her hand. "Come on. They're clean. You're literally shivering. Just go change, and I'll put your wet clothes in the dryer for you to change back into them later." He gave her mud-caked jeans a glance and added, "Okay, maybe the washer and *then* the dryer." As the storm redoubled its efforts and thunder roared overhead, he raised his voice and added, "I think we have time."

"All right," Sarah managed to say. "Thank you."

She went into the bathroom at the end of the hall, where she let her sopping wet jeans fall to the tile floor. Her skin was so wet under her clothes that she toweled off before getting dressed again. Even her bra had to go. At least the clothes he gave her were bulky – comfortable pajama pants and a thick sweatshirt. They were clean, but they still managed to smell like Adam. Damn it. He'd even included a pair of boxers to wear underneath. She wasn't sure if that was better or worse than going commando... but they sure were comfortable. She felt a faint stab of grief as she thought of how she used to wear Oliver's boxers around the house. It wasn't that she missed *him* so much... more that she missed the comfortable intimacy of being half of a married couple.

But enough of that. This wasn't the time for navel gazing. Sarah pulled on the pajama pants, rolling the waist several times to get them to fit a bit better. She had to get her clothes in the washer so that she could get out of here the moment the storm let up. Though given the state of her car and the continued noise on Adam's roof, that might not be before sunrise.

Was she really going to spend the night in Adam's house?!

She felt a momentary urge to call Todd and ask him to come save her, or to march out there and demand that Adam drive her the last few miles to Todd's house... but that would be selfish. The bathroom window rattled as another gust of wind seemed to shake the whole house. No, she couldn't do either one. Getting back out on the road right now would be irresponsible and wrong. So... where did that leave her?

Sarah surveyed the bathroom as she towel-dried her hair.

It was surprisingly clean, other than the pile of muddy clothes currently sitting in the middle of the tile floor. The bathroom sink was sparkling – not what she might have expected from a young guy who lived on his own. Then again, he probably had company often enough that he wanted to keep the place looking decent. Sarah's hand was on the doorknob when she noticed a bottle of cologne amongst Todd's other toiletries. She couldn't help but take a sniff.

That's when she got a good look at herself in the mirror. She looked like a drowned rat. Sarah groaned and turned off the bathroom light with some violence on her way out the door.

So she was stuck there for the time being. Sarah took a long, slow breath as she walked down the hallway. No biggie. It was just Adam. She'd known him for over a decade. He was Todd's best friend.

No.

Big.

Dealio.

Get a grip, Sarah.

Adam was in the kitchen, unpacking the sodden bag of groceries that had left a small puddle on his kitchen counter – not to mention a trail of water between there and the door. Sarah grabbed a towel to mop up the drips, along with the trail that she had left all the way down the hall on her way to the bathroom. She felt like a slug.

"Sorry for the mess," she muttered.

"It's just water," he said lightly, stashing her ice cream in the freezer. He was wearing a shirt now. That was a small mercy, she supposed.

"Where's your washing machine?"

"I'll throw your clothes in now," Adam said, though he didn't immediately hurry out of the kitchen. "I have a load to do anyway." He set a somewhat soggy box of mac and cheese on top of the six-pack of beer Sarah had chosen. "Now *this* is my idea of summer storm food. Thank God you showed up. I totally flaked on going to the store, and I was facing white bread and peanut butter for dinner. You really know how to get shut in for a storm, don't you? This is like my dream, end-of-days bunker-type food. Hope you plan to share?"

"Of course." Sarah poked at the wet cardboard box of mac and cheese, which was slightly slumped to one side. "I don't think most of this stuff will keep."

"Good thing these brownies are plastic wrapped. Dinner first? Or dessert?"

Sarah couldn't help but smile. She realized suddenly that she was *starving*. "I could use some real food before the sugar, I think."

Adam narrowed his eyes, still smirking. "Mac and cheese is more 'real food' than brownies?"

"*Obviously*," Sarah replied.

"Here." Adam pulled out a small pot, filled it with water, and set it on his stove. He lit the burner underneath it and said, "You start the macaroni, I'll start the laundry."

"How utterly domestic," Sarah muttered once he was safely out of earshot. She tossed a bit of salt into the water, then found a couple of glasses and poured each of them a beer. It was a good, dark local lager. She took a sip and felt her nerves settle, just a bit.

"Is that for me?" Adam asked as he walked back in.

"No," she told him with a straight face. "They're both mine."

"Motion denied." Adam picked up his glass and took a sip. "Wow, that's good!" He picked up one of the empty cans and examined it for a minute while Sarah poured the damp macaroni into the simmering water. Then he put the can down with a hollow *thunk* and asked, "Hey, where did you leave your car?"

"Just down the street," Sarah said. "Past Elm."

"You walked that far in *this*?" Adam gestured to the kitchen window, where the rain was pounding against the glass like it was demanding entry.

Sarah shrugged. "It was that or sleep in my car. My phone wasn't working."

"Well, I'm happy to be your safe harbor. I'll take a look at your car as soon as the rain lets up. If I can't get it running straight away, I'll have a tow truck come and take it to my garage in town."

"My aunt's boyfriend drives a tow truck. Beckett's Towing."

"Yeah, that's my guy! He's with your Aunt Anna?"

"Yep."

"Cool."

There was an awkward silence as Adam sipped his beer and Sarah checked the macaroni.

"Can we put on the weather channel?" she asked. "See if there will be a break in the storm?"

"Sure." But again, he wasn't in a hurry to leave the room. He was watching her with a focus that made her uneasy.

"Do you have milk and butter?" she asked. "For the cheese sauce."

"Sure do. Enough milk for brownies too." Adam opened his fridge and pulled out the dairy. "Remote's on the coffee table if you want to check the weather channel. I can finish up the feast."

Sarah smiled at him and went to check the weather forecast. A quick dinner with Adam wouldn't be so bad. Just don't let her be stuck here overnight, please... She prayed under her breath as the radar moved along the screen. No luck. It was just a wall of red until morning.

Unless she wanted to risk life and limb in that cat-three outside, she was stuck here.

All night long.

With Adam Tedeski.

Could this summer possibly get any more humiliating? As if in answer to her question, the light overhead seemed to flicker.

Sarah gasped. "Don't you dare."

Then, the room went dark.

God help her.

15

SARAH

"I found a couple more candles," Adam announced as he walked back into the living room. They had created a sort of hub around his coffee table, with pillows and blankets scattered across the floor. "Some other stuff too," he added, setting two boxes of board games and a deck of cards on the table. "In case we get bored after dinner."

Sarah couldn't imagine being bored when she felt like she was about to jump out of her skin. She seriously couldn't help but feel like the fates were playing a joke on her. How did this happen? Adam sat down across from her and set about lighting more candles. Sarah occupied herself with finishing the last of her lukewarm mac and cheese. Thank goodness Adam didn't have an electric stove. She wasn't sure she could have gotten even this far through the night without a big bowl of macaroni and cheese. As it was, she had half a mind to bolt out the door once the bowl was empty.

"Perfect," Adam said as he lit the last candle. His face was painfully handsome in the flickering light. Maybe Sarah should just call it quits and go to bed. It was nearly bedtime, right?

She checked her phone. It was five past six.

"Ready for brownies and milk?" Adam asked. Despite being wound tighter than a pocket watch, Sarah couldn't help but mirror his grin.

"I am always ready for brownies and milk," she enunciated. She was only two beers in, but she was a bit of a lightweight. A switch to milk was probably a good idea. Adam disappeared into the kitchen and returned shortly with generous servings of brownies and ice cream, then made another run into the kitchen for two tall glasses of milk. Once that was done, he gestured to the board games. He owned monopoly, some complicated murder mystery game that Sarah didn't recognize, and another game that was folded in half. It consisted of two wooden rectangles attached by a metal hinge.

"Is that mancala?" Sarah asked when she had swallowed her first huge bite of banana ice cream. "I haven't played since middle school."

Adam grinned and opened it up. Sure enough, it revealed the familiar depressions and colorful glass pieces of Sarah's favorite childhood game.

"You're on," she told him. Adam started an upbeat playlist going on his phone – Sarah had to admit, he had good taste in music – as she distributed the mancala pieces to their starting locations. They played a few games as they ate dessert, and slowly Sarah began to relax.

Why had she let herself get so worked up in the first place? It was nothing but a summer storm. So she happened to be riding out the storm with Adam. So what? She'd known the guy for half their lives. Why was she being so weird? Seeing him shirtless and sweaty hadn't made things any easier – but now that he was properly dressed, she could get through this night no problem. When they tired of mancala and Sarah wrinkled her nose at Adam's other games, he pulled out his laptop and offered her a long list of pirated movies that he'd downloaded years before. She chose a Will Ferrell movie that she hadn't seen since high school, and they kicked back on the couch with a couple more beers. Sarah tried not to read too much into how close Adam was, how he had chosen to sit shoulder-to-shoulder with her despite there being *plenty* of room on the other side of the couch. They were just watching on a little laptop screen, after all. No need to read into it. Still, she couldn't help but be excruciatingly aware of every spot where their bodies touched, the heat of his skin through their clothes, the low rumble of laughter through his chest... Sarah took another swig of her lager and tried to focus on the movie.

When Adam's laptop died midway through the second movie, he didn't move away. He put his feet up on the coffee table, nestling incrementally closer to Sarah in the process, and said, "How about a drinking game?" They were each on their fourth drink, at this point, a surprisingly good red wine that Adam had pulled out of his hat when they ran out of beer.

"What kind of drinking game?" Sarah asked cautiously.

"Two truths and a lie. Guess wrong, you drink. Guess right, the other person does."

"Okay," she relented. A stomach full of comfort food, topped with half of a six pack, had her feeling more agreeable than usual. "You go first."

Adam rattled his three off quickly. "I've never been to Canada, I'm terrified of heights, and I broke your Senorita Porky piggy bank when I was twelve."

"*You* broke my piggy bank?" Sarah exclaimed, sitting up straight.

Adam smiled at her from where he sat slouched on his sofa. "Is that your guess?"

"What?"

"You're supposed to guess which one is a lie."

"Oh." Sarah leaned back into the couch, keeping a few careful inches of space between her and Adam. "Right." She couldn't believe he had broken the ceramic pig that Aunt Anna had brought her from Mexico. It had been a beautiful, handmade piece of art, bright flowers on a white background, nearly full, with hundreds of dollars' worth of quarters. Sarah had blamed Jeff, who had sworn up and down that he had never touched her stupid pig.

She supposed it was just as well. She never would have had the heart to break the pig open to collect her money. Once she had recovered from the heartbreak of tossing the broken ceramic pieces into the garbage, she had rolled up the quarters and cashed them in for horseback riding lessons that summer.

"Hello? Earth to Sarah."

"A moment of silence for Senorita Porky," Sarah said grimly.

"Right," Adam agreed, matching her tone. "Of course."

Sarah nodded, letting the silence drag on a moment longer. Then, she said, "The Canada one. Obviously."

Adam gave her a wolfish smile. "Drink."

"What?" Sarah exclaimed. "You live in Maine! How have you never been to Canada?"

He shrugged, still grinning. "Drink."

Sarah took a sip of her wine, mind churning with the implications of his two truths and a lie. "But you're not afraid of heights. You and Todd used to go rock climbing all the time." She had gone with them more than once. The sight of Adam racing to the top of climbing walls or bouldering, muscles that no high school boy had any right to standing out starkly on his arms, had done nothing to quash the crush she had suffered from since early adolescence.

Adam just shrugged again, bright green eyes intent on Sarah's face. After a long moment, he said, "Wrong again. Drink."

Sarah's mouth fell open, and she put her glass down. "Now you're messing with me."

"I'm terrified of heights," he said earnestly. "I just don't let that stop me from doing the things that I want to do."

Sarah met his gaze until she risked losing herself in those leaf-green eyes. Then, she looked away and took another drink. "So you didn't break Senorita Porky?"

"I did not," he replied with mock gravity. "Your turn."

"Who broke my pig?"

Adam just laughed.

"It was Todd, wasn't it?"

He shrugged. "My mama didn't raise no snitches. Your turn."

"That brat." Sarah thought for a moment. Spurred on by the candlelight and Adam's own vulnerable honesty, she sought for a deeper offering than the surface-level things that sprang to mind.

"I've never gotten a C in my life, I'm scared of hummingbirds... and Oliver's the only person I've ever slept with."

Adam's expression was serious, and he regarded her for a long moment. Then, he smiled, but the expression held none of its usual irreverence. "Hummingbirds."

"Drink," Sarah commanded.

Adam's eyebrows rose and he took a long drink of his wine. When he lowered the glass, his expression had taken on a hint of its usual smirk. *"Hummingbirds?* Really?"

Sarah felt her forehead pull together. "They're like giant bugs. With superspeed. And daggers on their faces." Adam snorted, and she giggled. Maybe she'd had a *little* bit too much to drink.

"Okay. I guess I can see that."

"Care to take another guess?"

He met her eyes again, and Sarah's heart did a somersault. "Oliver?"

"Drink," Sarah said quietly, looking away. Why had she brought that up? She could feel her cheeks burning, and she felt slightly queasy with a vulnerability hangover. It was strange, hearing Adam say her husband's name. He wasn't even her ex-husband yet. Not officially. The paperwork was taking forever.

"You've gotten a C?" Adam quipped after taking a sip of wine. "I never would have guessed."

She smiled at him, grateful for the shift in focus. "High school physics," she admitted. "I got a C in the class and a two on the AP test. Got a five out of five on every other AP test I ever took, but I just could not grasp physics word problems to save my life. I had a tutor and everything. Just couldn't do it. Luckily, a C counts as a B for AP classes when they're calculating grade point average, so it didn't tank mine."

"I'm not sure that counts as a C," Adam teased gently. "Didn't you have like a four-point-seven GPA?"

"A C is a C," Sarah replied with a shrug. "I failed every physics test. Just couldn't wrap my head around how to apply the formulas to word problems. But the teacher gave us enough projects and extra credit assignments that I scraped by with a C."

"What sort of projects?" Adam asked.

"Egg drops, mouse trap cars, that sort of thing. I was good at those."

"You're good at most things." Adam's voice was a low rumble. His face seemed to be getting closer to hers. Sarah turned away and put her wine down. Maybe she was just starting to lose her sense of depth perception.

"Do you miss him?" Adam asked gently. "Oliver?"

"Sometimes," she admitted, still not looking at him. "Not as a husband, but as a... roommate, I guess? As a friend? At some point, we both realized that we cared deeply about each other, but we didn't make each other's hearts pound."

Adam leaned closer – she wasn't imagining it – and spoke into her ear, his voice very quiet.

"Do I make your heart pound, Sarah?"

The couch seemed to tilt beneath her. Adam's voice, his smell, his body heat... they were pulling her in like gravity. If it weren't for the rain still pounding on his roof, he would be able to *hear* her heart pound. Sarah turned her head, and her lips found his without even trying.

Everything disappeared.

Oliver, Val, Todd... for a long moment, none of them existed.

There was only the sound of the rain, Adam's lips on hers, Adam's hand on her leg, Adam's pulse pounding beneath her fingers as her hand rested on his neck...

And then, Sarah pulled away, gasping.

What was she *doing*?

Something she would surely regret in the morning, that's what.

She nearly fell off the couch, caught herself on the coffee table and managed to stand.

"I'm super exhausted," she said, though in truth her pounding heart and the adrenaline in her veins had her feeling anything but. "Is it okay if I go to sleep?"

Adam stared at her for a second, lips parted slightly in surprise. Then, he managed a facsimile of his usual teasing smile and said, "Of course. The guest room is to the right of the bathroom."

"Okay." Sarah backed away. She was having a hard time tearing her eyes from Adam's face. Honestly, she was having a hard time not closing the space between them, climbing onto his lap where he sat on the couch, disheveled and beautiful, a yearning look in his eyes that his smile couldn't quite hide – *Get a grip, Sarah.* She forced herself to turn away, walk out of the room, and splash cold water on her face at the bathroom sink.

She stood in the hallway for a long moment. Her hand was on the doorknob that led to the guest room. Her eyes were on the door across the hall. Adam's door.

In the end, she went into the guest room and closed the door behind her.

It was all too overwhelming. *He* was all too overwhelming.

Adam had been nothing but a needless distraction ever since her return to Bluebird Bay. She had run into all sorts of trouble simply because her head wasn't in the game. Sarah was on the path to success. She always had been. And if she wanted to be a success in life, she couldn't afford this sort of distraction.

Sarah climbed into the cushy guest bed, so cold in contrast to their candlelit nook on the couch. As the wind howled outside her window, she wondered why she felt so terribly alone.

16

FALLYN

"I know you two are busy as a pair of beavers working, so I'll be out of your way in a jiffy, but I figured you must be needing some fuel by now."

Molly's bell-like voice rang through the great room, and Fallyn turned her gaze from the easel she and David had set up in front of the fireplace. No oil paints in sight, unfortunately. Just a mess of blurry pictures and house layouts and other puzzle pieces that just didn't seem to fit together. They were due for a lunch break.

"Perfect timing, actually," Fallyn said with a grateful smile as her gaze locked on the tray of lunch meats and freshly baked five-grain bread. Molly was a talented baker, and Fallyn had been lucky enough to be on the receiving end of her food since arriving in Bluebird Bay.

"And please," David added, "don't worry about interrupting us, ma'am. We're the ones imposing by taking up your living room."

"Pish posh," Molly said brightly. "The room just sits empty all day. I'm either reading my stories at the front desk or cooking up a storm in the kitchen. You're welcome to use this space anytime you'd like."

"That's very kind," David said with his characteristic seriousness. "Thank you."

"My pleasure. You enjoy your food now, and let me know if you need anything else. Actually, hold that thought. I forgot your mustard."

Fallyn and David exchanged a smile as Molly bustled out of the room. Half the town was without power the morning after the storm, including David's home and his office. When he had told Fallyn that morning that both places weren't likely to be reconnected to the grid until the next day at the earliest, she'd invited him to the inn to work. The idea had been to set up in her room – but when Fallyn had mentioned to Molly at breakfast that David was coming, Molly had offered the living room in her own personal quarters towards the back of the inn for them to use so that they could spread out and be comfortable. Despite Fallyn's attempts to decline, she wouldn't take no for an answer. They'd been at it for hours now, and Fallyn was grateful for the borrowed space. At least here they had room to stretch their legs and change seats every so often without feeling cramped. Better yet? The refreshments.

"This is quite a spread," David said. He was slathering some sort of soft, herb-studded cheese onto a warm slice of bread.

"I've put on a few pounds since moving here," Fallyn admitted, half laughing.

David gave her a long look. "You wear them well."

Fallyn's cheeks were burning as Molly came back into the room with a dish of mustard and other condiments, including a spicy relish that she and her daughter made each summer.

"Thank you," David said earnestly. "This is an amazing meal."

"Oh, it's just a thrown-together lunch platter," Molly told him. "I love making people at home, and I love being in the kitchen. It's really no bother."

"You picked the right career, then."

"I was born for this," she said agreeably. Her gaze drifted towards their board, with its fuzzy security-camera photos and maps and lists of names. "I'm happy to help where I can. You're doing important work here, and that takes fuel. It must be exciting, solving real-life mysteries like this."

David put the finishing touches on his sandwich and took a bite. After he swallowed, he said, "This might be the best lunch I've had in my entire life. Certainly the best bread I've tasted since my Meemaw passed away."

"You're too sweet." Molly looked away from the board and smiled at David. "You two enjoy. I'll be back in a bit with dessert."

Dessert? David mouthed at Fallyn as Molly walked away. The door closed and he said, "I may have to get rid of my place and think about moving in here."

Fallyn smiled at him and turned her attention to her own complicated tower of a sandwich that was midway through construction. He was only teasing – and a good thing, too. It occurred to her that it would be particularly difficult for her to get a good night's sleep with David Shaw just down the hall.

"Molly's a gem," he said. "And I wasn't lying about the bread. This is incredible."

"She's the sweetest," Fallyn agreed. "It was hard for me to get used to at first."

"What do you mean?" David asked.

"Molly's a hugger and a nurturer. That's just... out of my wheelhouse, I guess."

"Your mom wasn't a hugger?" he asked gently.

"You could say that." Fallyn's voice was dry. "I can hardly remember her touching me, much less the constant hugs that moms like Molly dole out. My mother is... reserved. And I guess I got used to that, because I still struggle sometimes with, well, physical touch. A certain level of intimacy and it's hard for me not to feel smothered. Even with someone as amazing as Molly."

"Very good to know," David rumbled.

Fallyn's cheeks flamed, and she deliberately avoided David's gaze as she put the finishing touches on her masterpiece of a sandwich. They were quiet as they ate, and Fallyn reflected that that was one of her favorite things about David. The man could hold up his end of a conversation without a problem, but he didn't feel the need to fill the air with idle talk. They were able to enjoy long, comfortable silences too. And that was even more rare than stimulating conversation.

"Me again," Molly called out, coming back into the room just as they were finishing their sandwiches. "I hope you saved room for dessert."

"Not really," Fallyn laughed, "but your desserts are so scrumptious that I'll have some anyway."

"I brought some black coffee too, to balance out the heavy food. We have lemon pound cake today, with a drizzle of blackberry sauce on top."

"That sounds amazing," David said. "Thank you."

"My pleasure." Molly set the new tray down and picked up the old one. She straightened and then paused, her eye catching on the board that Fallyn and David had been working on all morning. "I know that name."

David cocked his head. "Which one?"

"Charles Ericson. In fact, I'm mortified to admit that I still have about a hundred cases of the diet supplement he convinced me to buy about ten years back. They're down in the cellar somewhere. What a fool I was." Molly was wearing a frown that looked strange on her ever-pleasant face. "I swear that man could sell sand in a desert."

Fallyn and David exchanged a look, and David picked up his notebook.

"What was the name of the supplement, if you don't mind me asking?"

Molly thought for a moment. "SkinniQuick, I think it was called. Powdered stuff. Tasted like death. I never did manage to sell any of it. Couldn't even stomach it myself past the first week." Molly shrugged and her smile reappeared, still somewhat dimmer than usual. "Oh well. You live and you learn, that's what I always say. I'll leave you to it, shall I?"

Fallyn snatched up her laptop as Molly left the room.

"Here it is," she said after a few minutes of searching. "SkinniQuick. It's been off the market for nine years. Company disappeared around the same time, it looks like."

"Look at this." David turned his own laptop in Fallyn's direction. "I found an old infomercial."

"Breaking news!" announced a thin woman in her twenties. Her hair was slicked back and she was wearing a dark blazer. "This new supplement is sweeping the nation!

By replacing just one meal a day with SkinniQuick, any excess weight that you've been carrying will fall right off! We have a resident expert here in the studio to tell us more."

"Thanks, Brooke." Fallyn knew that voice... sure enough, the camera cut to Charles Ericson, ten years younger and fifty pounds lighter. Already bald as the day they met him, though.

"I'll be damned," David muttered.

Charles talked for a solid five minutes about this new miracle product that was changing lives. Beyond being a health-promoting wonder, he claimed it to be a phenomenal business opportunity.

"You have the chance to get in on the ground floor," he said seriously, looking directly into the camera. "You can make your community healthier and get paid to do it. It's a win-win."

It was *not* a pyramid scheme, he emphasized, but rather a revolutionary reverse trickle-down model in which the money moved upwards in a cyclical fashion.

As he droned on about what a unique supplement and phenomenal opportunity this was for anyone looking for a secondary stream of income that would quickly outstrip their primary income, Fallyn kept digging. She used a website called the Way Back Wizard to look up defunct social media pages for SkinniQuick. By the time the infomercial was over, she had found references to *five* more people who had been robbed. They all had sold SkinniQuick around the same time as Charles.

"That's not nothing," David murmured when she showed him. "Any lawsuits?"

They dug around for a good hour, but they couldn't find

any evidence of lawsuits or other backlash against the company. It seemed that SkinniQuick had just quietly disappeared.

"Maybe people were embarrassed," Fallyn mused.

"Look at this," David said, turning his screen to face her. "The company filed for bankruptcy nine years ago. Everything went quiet after that."

"Strange that they would file for bankruptcy when everyone involved is still so wealthy."

"It happens more than you'd think. Some people file for bankruptcy deliberately, on a regular basis. Manipulative debt reduction. It wipes the slate clean."

"That's crazy."

David shrugged. "It's a broken system."

Fallyn was still clicking through old social media posts as she ate Molly's incredible lemon pound cake. Her whole body was buzzing with the combination of phenomenal food and a promising lead.

"We're onto something, David."

"I know we are," he agreed quietly, clicking through information on his own computer. His phone started to buzz, and he looked at Fallyn with raised eyebrows. "It's Charles Ericson."

David's cell wasn't on speakerphone, but Fallyn could still hear Charles from several feet away. His voice rose and fell as Fallyn caught words like *incompetent* and *disappointed.* David held the phone away from his ear with a look of distaste and put it on speaker.

"*Another* robbery just days before the storm. Clearly we hired the wrong man for the job if this is still going on."

"When did Mrs. Amberger realize that her things were missing?" David asked calmly.

"When she got back home today. They rode out the storm at a friend's place in Newport. She went to put some jewelry back in her box and that's when she realized her best pearls were gone. That's when Freddie checked his safe. *Fifty thousand dollars* worth of rare coins, gone. We've had it with your incompetence, Shaw. Freddie's threatening to sue the both of us, since I'm the fool who hired you. You have forty-eight hours to prove him wrong while *I* try to find someone who knows what the hell he's doing. If you can't solve this case by then, you're out on your ass."

"Understood," David said, and hung up. He looked at Fallyn with one eyebrow raised.

"Well then," Fallyn said, "let's dig a little deeper into Mr. Ericson's dirty laundry and see if we're right."

As they got back on the trail, Fallyn couldn't help but wonder if Charles Ericson would end up wishing this was a mystery they had never dug into.

17

SARAH

Sarah felt pleasantly tired after a day of physical work. Everybody had pitched in to get Steph's house and yard cleaned up after the storm, and Sarah had worked up a good appetite. She helped herself to a second piece of lemon-miso salmon and another big scoop of Anna's salad as her brothers bickered over the last dinner roll.

"I should get it," Jeff insisted. "I did most of the work."

Todd snorted. "You milked that backyard limb cleanup for*ever*. It could have taken an *hour* and you were out there all day. Getting the mud out of Mom's wheel wells and power washing the driveway was way more work."

"Than moving fallen branches?" Jeff exclaimed. "Are you kidding me?"

"You spent most of your time *admiring* the branches."

"They're salvageable! That's good hardwood."

"Whatever." Todd reached for the roll, but Anna was quicker. She tore the roll in half and Jeff shot Todd a grin. Todd ignored him, but he shrugged and reached out for the roll, looking appeased. Then, Anna put one half on Steph's plate and popped the other half in her mouth. Whole. Sarah snorted as her mom full-out laughed at the shocked looks on Todd and Jeff's faces.

"No fair!" Todd said with comically exaggerated outrage.

Anna rolled her eyes, swallowed her gargantuan bite, and said, "So you all came over to help your old, decrepit mother put things back together after the hurricane. What, you think you should get a Nobel Peace Prize or something now? *She* taught three yoga classes and then came home and made you this feast." She shot her big sister a warning look and said, "You had better not give either of them that roll."

Steph raised an eyebrow. "While I object to being cast as the old decrepit mother in this scenario," she said drolly as she buttered the dinner roll, "I agree with the rest of your assessment."

"Rude," Jeff muttered, slouching back in his chair.

Steph bit into the roll with a teasing groan. Anna laughed as Jeff scrunched up his face.

Silly family dynamics and bickering brothers notwithstanding, Sarah was glad that she came today. Being in her childhood home surrounded by family felt deeply comfortable after a stressful storm, and the cleanup had been a welcome distraction from thoughts of the night before.

That *night*...

Sarah pushed an olive around her plate as she thought about her time with Adam. That *kiss*... ugh. And her awkward escape into the guest bedroom... It was just a no-win scenario. She could kick that boy for backing her into a corner with his charm and his overblown hospitality.

He was gone when she woke up in the morning, and she had called Todd first thing to ask him to come pick her up.

She had pulled her own clothes out of Adam's dryer – they were all mixed up with his t-shirts, a pair of his boxers clinging to her jeans – and changed, trying not to feel like she was preparing for a walk of shame. Nothing had happened, after all.

Well... almost nothing.

Todd had just pulled into the driveway when Adam came walking up the road. He had been looking at her car, but said that he wouldn't be able to fix it that day. He would have it towed to his shop and order the part that needed to be replaced. Sarah hadn't really grokked the details. She had been so preoccupied with trying to act normal in front of her brother. And she hadn't quite managed it. When she thought back on how quickly she had jumped into his Jeep and the odd look Todd had given her – not to mention the stilted tone of voice he had used to thank his friend for putting Sarah up for the night – she wanted to crawl into bed and stay there for a week.

Not that she *had* a bed. In that one respect, staying at Adam's place had been a welcome change from Todd's couch.

If she hadn't been so distracted, she never would have let Adam take charge of fixing her car. It meant that she had to go see him again in a couple days. What was she going to say to him? Tell him that she wasn't ready for another relationship? Not that that's what Adam was looking for... Was she supposed to just pretend like that kiss – that *kiss!* – had never happened?

She did the right thing, stopping things from going any further. She had no idea what the future held for her, but it couldn't possibly center on a guy like Adam. Sarah might take life a little too seriously sometimes, but Adam had never taken life seriously *enough*.

She already felt like a failure, going through a divorce halfway through her twenties. With Adam, failure was almost a surety. Wasn't it?

Adam was like that storm that had tossed them together. He was a force to be reckoned with. Wild, untamed, leaving a mile-wide trail of wreckage in his wake. Worse, he made Sarah feel things that terrified her. He made her feel out of control when she worked so hard to keep her life steady and safe.

If she let Adam sweep her away, she would likely end up like the rickety shed she and Jeff had cleaned up a couple of hours before. Wrecked.

"You sure you're okay?" Todd asked. Sarah jumped. Her big brother was leaning towards her, keeping his voice low. "You seem a little off today."

"I'm fine," she said, slightly snappish. He had asked her that question three times already.

Her brother had been awkwardly silent for most of the car ride that morning, until just before he turned onto the street they grew up on. With their childhood home looming in the distance, he had asked if anything had happened between Adam and Sarah the night before.

"No," she had said reflexively. "Nothing. What are you talking about?"

"I just," he started, then shook his head as he parked in front of their mom's house. "Nothing. Good."

"Good?" she had challenged, feeling miffed that he felt she had to answer to him at all.

"It would just be really awkward for me, you know? My best friend and my sister... yuck."

"Well, you don't even need to go there," she'd told him as she jumped over a puddle to get out of his Jeep, "because it's never going to happen."

Slamming the door as hard as she had probably hadn't done much to set his mind at ease. He'd been giving her weird looks all day, and she had been avoiding him as best as she could, helping Jeff with branch cleanup or helping Mom in the kitchen.

"I just have a lot on my mind," she told him now. "I'm starting my life from scratch, okay? People act like it should be easier since I'm basically just coming home again, but if anything, that just makes it harder. Navigating all of the questions is overwhelming. I can't even go to the grocery store without people asking me what I plan to do with my life. It makes me feel like a kid again, and I hate it."

Belatedly, Sarah realized that the rest of the family had stopped talking and turned to listen to her vent her frustrations. Which was the absolute last thing she wanted.

It was all enough to make a girl decide to pick up and move to Florida.

"You could let me help with the house hunt," Steph suggested gently. "I can ask around and find out if there's something available that isn't listed online. We could go look together? It could be fun."

"Sure," Sarah said, forcing a smile. "Thank you. It will be fun."

It broke her heart to hear the tenuous tone in her mother's voice each time she spoke to her these days, as if she were walking on eggshells to avoid offending her and driving her away. Sarah's secrecy over the slow dissolution of her marriage and her decision to stay with Todd instead of moving home had created a breach between her and Steph that might take some time to mend. House hunting together would go a long way towards mending fences and finding their footing in this new relationship of a mother and her adult daughter living in the same town. Anyway, Sarah's mom had great taste in homes. And between her long-established veterinary practice and her new vocation of part-time yoga teacher, Steph knew just about everybody in Bluebird Bay.

"How's the job hunt going?" Anna asked.

"I got a couple job offers this week," Sarah said.

Anna grinned. "Of course you did."

The big firm had called that morning when she was working outside, just like she had known they would. And Val's offer had been on her mind every day. But the truth was, neither job was taking up as much headspace as Adam was. What was *wrong* with her?

"Tell us about them," Anna said, pulling Sarah back out of her thoughts.

"They're very different," Sarah said. "One is an established firm that's located in the Myer's Building."

"Excellent food. Very important consideration. Go on."

Sarah smiled, forgetting her worries for the moment. Her Aunt Anna had that effect on people.

"It's run by three women," Sarah continued.

"Very cool."

"I like them a lot. I think it would be a good job. They handle a lot of corporate clients, but they're mostly small businesses. Some mergers and stuff. It's not stuff that I have a lot of experience with, but I know I could get up to speed quickly. And it would be interesting, I think."

"Sounds awesome. What's the other job?"

"It's riskier," Sarah said. "It doesn't even really exist yet."

"How intriguing." Anna leaned forward, planting her elbows on either side of her empty dinner plate. "Tell me more."

Sarah smiled again, even though she *knew* that Anna was hamming it up to get her out of her funk. Or maybe *because* she knew that's what her aunt was doing.

"Val Rodolphi is starting her own local firm. Her plan is to be a general practice attorney, so the firm would cover most of the things that people in town need on a regular basis. Everything from leases to litigation. She wants to work on a sliding scale and even take on pro bono stuff where she can. It's a really lovely idea, but it's definitely a risk."

"Does she have a solid business plan?" Steph asked.

Sarah turned to look at her mom. "She does, actually. She already has a location and an impressive list of clients. More than she can comfortably manage and still have time to spend with her kid. Which is where I would come in."

"Splitting the case load with Corey at the clinic was a lifesaver," Todd said. "Trying to run that place on my own was exhausting. I can't imagine trying to do that *and* raise a kid."

"Yeah, she'll need a partner," Sarah said. "I'm just not sure if I'm the right person for the job."

"Of course not," Todd said. "You're not a risk taker."

She frowned at him. "What are you talking about?"

"You play it safe, that's all."

"It's the flip side of being a perfectionist," Steph said in that new, timid tone she had taken to using with her daughter. "You take on things you know you can do well and you persevere until you can get them right. But if something doesn't come to you easily, like drawing or singing, then you don't do it at all. It doesn't mean you can't start your own firm. I know you can. It just means that you won't do it with Val unless you're sure that you can make a go of it."

Todd added, "Don't leave Val dangling too long if you're just going to take the other job. Which you are."

If there had been any dinner rolls left, Sarah might have thrown one at his head.

"What do you mean *dangling too long*? She *just* sent me the business proposal!"

"We're a family of risk takers," Anna said stoutly. "Just look at how many entrepreneurs we have in the family. Every one of the Sullivan sisters and both of Cee-cee's kids. Now, you're running your mom's clinic and Jeff is on his way to become a master carpenter. Why should Sarah be any different?"

"I don't know why," Todd said, overtly teasing now, "but she always has been."

"Remember the lemonade stand?" Jeff put in, grinning. "We put days into building it, but then Saturday rolled around and you backed out."

"I didn't back out," Sarah grumbled. "I told you that we should wait for another day because the weather was too cold."

"You didn't want to take the risk," Jeff said triumphantly.

Sarah rolled her eyes. "It wasn't a *risk*. It was a waste of time. It was cold and windy that day. You made, what, like, six dollars? Even at ten, my labor was worth more than thirty cents an hour."

Everyone laughed – even Sarah, a second after the rest of them. Maybe they were right. She had never been much of a risk taker. But she was a hard worker. Once she set her mind to something, she accomplished it. Rain or shine. Not including the stupid lemonade stand when she was *ten*, which she *would* have taken out the next sunny Saturday if *someone* hadn't dismantled it to try and build himself a go-cart.

"There's nothing wrong with taking time to mull it over." Steph squeezed Sarah's shoulder on her way into the kitchen for the pie they had made together that afternoon.

"Even when we all know what you're going to do," Jeff needled her.

Sarah busied herself with clearing the table before dessert, trying not to let her brothers' teasing get to her. Was she really a chicken?

So what if she was.

At least she was a smart chicken.

18

CEE-CEE

Cee-cee finished installing the final drawer handle and stood up, stretching this way and that to ease the stiffness in her lower back. Max was just finishing up the last of her stenciling. They had painted the cabinets white to bring some light into the small apartment kitchen, and Max had added some whimsical flair and color with stencils she'd ordered online. For Cee-cee, the day's work had been all about spending time with her daughter. Between tourist season at the cupcake shop and spending most of her free time with baby Grace, she hadn't seen much of Max the past few weeks, but she had to admit, the kitchen looked amazing. It never ceased to amaze her how drastically a day's work and a coat of paint could transform a space.

"Ian's going to be so surprised," Max said as she finished her final bit of stenciling, a spattering of flowers at the bottom of one of the cabinet doors. "We've been talking about painting these cupboards for months, but he's always working so hard on the newest escape room that I think even the thought of having to come home and paint, sand, or saw something makes him twitchy."

"It looks beautiful, Max."

"Thanks, Mom." Max rose to her feet with none of Cee-cee's stiffness and pulled her into a hug. "I couldn't have done it without you. Knocked this project out in a single day, I mean. You're the best."

Cee-cee held her daughter close and then released her when she began to squirm. Max turned back towards the newly painted cabinets and regarded their work with a beaming smile. As Cee-cee regarded her daughter's beautiful, paint-speckled face, a wave of unexpected nausea rolled over her.

Your daughter has never been so happy, and you want to blow it all up on some hunch? she thought incredulously. *Why would you do anything that could cause her that sort of heartache?*

Cee-cee tried to push away thoughts of Nate and his probable connection to the disappearance of Emily Addison. She didn't want to think about *any* of that today. She just wanted to be present in this moment, this rare treat of a whole day alone with her only daughter.

Max had moved on from the cabinets. She was washing her hands in the kitchen sink and talking with animated excitement about her latest estate-sale haul of antique books. Cee-cee had been too distracted to follow the details, but she smiled and nodded when Max looked at her. Max dried her hands and Cee-cee took her turn at the sink, working to calm and center herself.

Deep breaths, Cee-cee. Just be here now.

"You have to see them," Max continued, still beaming. "I'm going to grab them. Be right back."

Max came stomping down the apartment staircase a minute later carrying a heavy stack of books. She set them on Ian's glass coffee table and Cee-cee knelt on the plush rug beneath to take a closer look. She didn't share Max's passion for old books, but she had to admit that Max's latest finds were really stunning. Most of them were leather-bound, dyed rich shades of red and blue and green. Some were even embossed with gold leaf. The covers were beautiful, but some of them were falling apart. Max handled them carefully, showing Cee-cee pages that had come loose and explaining how she was going to restore them so that they were whole and readable again. One of many skills Max had honed in the past couple of years, Cee-cee reflected with a familiar surge of pride and affection.

"I have something else to show you," Max said as she carefully closed the book they had been looking at and returned it to the stack of antiques. "I thought about waiting until it was finished, but I'm just too excited. And I want your feedback."

Max went to one of her many bookshelves and fetched an old-fashioned scrapbook. It was custom made, with the words *Amazing Grace* embossed on the cover. Cee-cee found herself blinking back tears as Max opened it to a picture of Grace sleeping in Cee-cee's arms.

"Oh, Maxy. What a lovely thing to do for Sasha and Gabe."

"I'm going to give it to them on Gracie's first birthday," Max told her. "I stole an ultrasound photo off Gabe and

Sasha's fridge, and Aunt Anna's taken thousands of pictures of Grace. Some pregnancy shots of Sasha too."

Cee-cee flipped through the book slowly, astonished by the amount of care and detail that Max had put into making it. The book contained so much more than just pictures. Each photo was captioned with gorgeous calligraphy. There were poems, hand-pressed flowers, doodles... Max had even included Gabe and Sasha's wedding photo and a photo of them on the beach the summer they'd started dating. The first page had a baby photo of Gabe, who looked nothing at all like his delicate baby girl. He had been a tank. Cee-cee's arms still remembered the weight of him, his head heavy on her shoulder. Watching her children grow was so bittersweet.

"I don't have a baby picture of Sasha," Max said, "and I didn't want to ruin the surprise, but I left room for one. I thought I could include a section near the end for everyone in the family to write Gracie a note about the first year of her life, including a blank page for Gabe and Sash to fill in after I give it to them. Do you think they'll like it?"

"Maxy," Cee-cee said, her voice cracking with emotion, "they're going to *love* it. I love it. It's the most beautiful, thoughtful gift I have ever seen in my life. I would be honored to add my own little love letter to Gracie."

"Good." Max smiled and closed the book gently. "There are still plenty of blank pages. I wanted to make sure to leave enough room. She's growing and changing so fast."

"Babies do that," Cee-cee murmured. There was a strand of dark hair drifting close to Max's eye, clumped together with a dollop of white paint, and Cee-cee brushed it back behind her daughter's ear.

"Gabe's an amazing dad," Max marveled. "It's crazy to

see how much he's grown up now that he has his own little family. He's so patient and steady. And Sasha's a natural mom. Gracie's really lucky to have them. And you."

"She's lucky to have all of us," Cee-cee agreed. "Almost as lucky as we are to have her."

"I need to pee," Max announced, jumping back to her feet, "and then I should put in our takeout order for Ian to grab on his way home. Are you staying for dinner?"

"Not tonight. I told Mick I'd get us something from the diner."

"Okay," Max said agreeably. She turned and trotted back up the stairs, and Cee-cee watched her go with a smile. She appreciated the invitation, even if it had been somewhat halfhearted. She knew that Max would rather spend the evening alone with her boyfriend than have her mother stay on after being there all day. The young couple worked such crazy, entrepreneurial hours that their time together was a carefully guarded commodity.

She understood that better than most women her age. She spent less time with Mick than she might like, and each hour was precious to her. They had promised each other that by next summer, they would each delegate enough work to their employees to cut their own weekly hours down below forty.

Cee-cee opened the scrapbook again, staring down at a picture of Nate holding their shared granddaughter. His smile was photo-perfect, with none of the stress Cee-cee saw on his face each time they ran into each other. Was he only nervous around *her*?

Their lives were so utterly perfect this summer. Why

would she go and ruin it all by causing stress and strife with Gracie's grandfather?

So Nate was acting strange. So what? He hadn't been himself in years. Between their divorce and his own catastrophic financial decisions, he had been a stress case ever since their split. She was jumping to ridiculous conclusions, linking her ex-husband to the cold-case murder that had shocked their community earlier that year. Surely, Nate's off behavior was just more evidence of him spiraling after his financial missteps, just a symptom of his failure to come to grips with their divorce. He didn't know how to act around her anymore, this new and improved Cee-cee two-point-oh. There was no need to cause drama just when things were going so beautifully for everyone else in the family.

Nate would right the ship and come out on top. Guys like Nate always did. Appearances were everything to him. Cee-cee should just mind her own business and give the man a wide berth while he figured things out.

Max and Cee-cee made small talk for a while as they cleaned up the kitchen. They had just finished when Ian got home bearing bags of Chinese food. He kissed Max on the forehead and headed for the kitchen to put the food down, then froze mid-step.

"Did you do this?" he exclaimed. "Max, this looks amazing!"

"Me and Mom," Max confirmed.

Ian put the food down on the counter and crouched to examine the detail work.

"Does the stenciling look okay?" Max asked, scrunching her nose the way she did when she was nervous. She had made that face ever since she was a little girl.

Ian stood again and pulled Max into a hug that lifted her feet from the floor. "It's perfect, Max. I love it. Thank you, Cee-cee," he added, grinning at her over the top of Max's head. "You're the best. I'm so grateful that I didn't have to do it. I've been working on the Halloween rooms night and day, so our apartment always gets the short end of the stick. I've had zero energy for home improvement projects."

"I was happy to help," Cee-cee told him.

"Will you stay for dinner?" Ian asked. "We have enough for six people. Leftovers keep us going."

"Thanks, but no. I told Mick I'd bring him fish and chips from Mo's Diner, and he'll be done with work soon. You two enjoy."

Max gave her one last squeeze before she left, and Cee-cee's heart was light as she drove the short distance to the diner. The place was bustling, and Cee-cee made small talk with some of her own regular customers as she stood waiting for her food.

"Cee-cee!" a familiar voice exclaimed. Maryanne Carpenter Brown pulled Cee-cee into a hug the moment she turned to look at her. Her beau Alex stood at her shoulder; when Maryanne released her, he held out his hand for Cee-cee to shake.

"I see an open table," he murmured to Maryanne. "I'll go grab it. You stay and chat. No rush."

"Thanks," Maryanne said. She watched Alex as he walked away, and there was a softness to her expression that Cee-cee had never seen there before. Then, she turned back to Cee-cee with a smile and asked how her summer was going.

"Good," Cee-cee told her. "Busy. Between the shop and

my new grandbaby, I have hardly any free time at all. But that suits me just fine." She pulled out her phone and showed Maryanne her latest pictures of Gracie; the other woman oohed and aahed for a polite amount of time before straightening up and changing the subject.

"Hey, is Mick as busy as you are right now?"

"Pretty much. Business is booming for both of us. Why?"

"I was wondering if he might be able to spare Jeff for a couple days. I need a fence around my rose garden. My neighbor's Labradoodle pup is the cutest thing you have ever seen, but she keeps running right through their invisible fence. I don't know if her electric collar is faulty or if the creature is some kind of masochist, but she loves to go tearing through my herb garden and then try to dig up my new rose bushes."

Cee-cee chuckled. "I'll ask him. I'm sure he can work something out. How has everything else been?" She shot a glance to Alex, who was considerably kinder and better looking than any other man she had seen Maryanne with over the years. But when she looked back at Maryanne, she was surprised to see a look of grief on the other woman's face.

"Life is good," she said immediately, trying for a bright smile and almost succeeding. It faded as she said, "Alex is wonderful. I just wish the circumstances had been different, you know? It's hard to have the best part of my life and the worst thing to ever happen to this town all tied up together."

Cee-cee swallowed hard and nodded. Her stomach sank as she remembered Alex's connection to the Addison family. That shared connection was the only reason that he and Maryanne had met, and they had gotten together just as the truth of Emily's disappearance had surfaced.

Maryanne continued, "We had hoped that finally laying Emily to rest would help Patty somehow. It seems silly now. We had it in our heads that it would help bring her back to the present, help her be less confused. *Something*. But she's just fading away. The last few times I've visited her, she's been unresponsive. Not raging or out of control or anything. Just... staring out into space. Not really there. I think that something broke inside of her when she realized that Emily was lost for good, that neither of her children are ever coming back. There's just no fixing a thing like that."

"No," Cee-cee agreed, her voice almost inaudible. "There isn't."

Just then, Eva came over with her fish and chips. The smell of the fried food made Cee-cee's already queasy stomach roil.

"Thanks, Eva," she said quickly. "Good to see you, Maryanne. Sorry, I've got to run. Enjoy your dinner."

She rushed to the front doors and shoved them open, taking a deep breath of the moderately cooler air outside. Her heart was pounding, and she still felt like she might puke right there on the sidewalk. Aware of Maryanne's eyes on her through the glass, Cee-cee turned and forced herself to walk down the street towards her apartment. The thought of poor Patty Addison and what had happened to her daughter would haunt Cee-cee for all of her days if she tried to bury her suspicions beneath the floorboards of her mind. It was no use. She wouldn't be able to live with herself if she didn't speak out about her suspicions.

She just hoped that she would be able to live with the fallout...

19

SARAH

"Maybe we should just call it for the day, Mom," Sarah muttered miserably as Steph pulled the car back onto the road.

She was exhausted, both mentally and emotionally. After a heartfelt and melancholy conversation with Oliver earlier that morning, they'd signed the final divorce papers. She wasn't sad about that, but it had been emotional. Then, she and her mother had gone off home-hunting. Probably not the best timing...

The last place had been just about perfect, but the price was closer to what she would expect for a place in DC than what she had thought she would be paying to rent a one-bedroom in Bluebird Bay.

"Either I'm not in the right frame of mind to see the pros and cons of each of these places properly, or my budget needs to be reworked."

Stephanie reached over and squeezed her hand. "I won't argue that you're not exactly a bouquet of roses and sunshine today, but to my mind, none of those places were worth the money they were asking. Let's just look at this next one, all right? The location is perfect, and it's only a few minutes down the road."

Sarah nodded and hunkered down lower in her seat. "Okay. Last one, though."

Her mom was right. She was in a mood. Ever since dinner the night before, her brother's words had been haunting her.

You're not a risk taker. You play it safe.

Bold words from the man who had inherited the business that their mother had built from the ground up. He had followed in Steph's footsteps while Sarah had blazed a trail that was utterly unlike anything that anyone in their family had done before her. She had worked with a Supreme Court Justice, for Pete's sake! And he had the nerve to pretend that he knew her better than she knew herself. Talk about projecting. Todd wasn't exactly a risk taker himself.

But Sarah had to be honest with herself: his words had stuck with her because there was at least some truth to them. If Val's business panned out, it was exactly the sort of thing that Sarah would love to get in on the ground floor of. She could see herself devoting her life to a business like that. The variety would keep her work from getting dull, and she loved the idea of giving back to the community that had raised her with pro bono work.

But it wasn't a sure thing. And the other job was just as appealing. Or... nearly.

Was she a coward for turning down the beautiful apartment that was just beyond her budget? Signing a lease before she'd landed a job felt foolish... but that wasn't cowardice. It was just good common sense.

And Adam? asked a voice in the back of her mind.

What about him? she shot back. He was nothing but a distraction. And Sarah was nothing to *him* but a passing amusement. Never mind how much he'd been *on* her mind. She was not about to jump into a rebound fling with her brother's best friend.

Though if she did, it would serve Todd right for acting like he knew what she was going to do before she had made a decision...

"One one seven," Steph said, pulling Sarah out of the haze of her thoughts. She looked out the window as her mom parked the car – and once she realized where they were, she sat up a little straighter. There was a little spit of beach visible just off to the right; she could see a stretch of ocean sparkling beneath blue sky. And despite the mess of tree branches and other wreckage from the storm, the property was inviting. Instead of a flat expanse of lawn, the front yard was a riot of tall native grasses and summer flowers. If it still looked this beautiful after a storm, she could only imagine how lovely and fragrant it must be on a good day. The cottage beyond the flowers was like something out of a picture book, with worn white walls and old-fashioned paneled windows.

"Was this the one that said it needed work?" she asked, leafing through the pile of papers in her lap. She let the printouts for the apartments and condos fall to the ground as she looked at the listing for the cottage in front of them. No, not a listing. An email from a friend of her mom's who lived down the street. Phenomenal location. One bedroom. Just over six hundred square feet. Practically perfect in every way – particularly the price point. Probably too good to be true...

"That's the one," her mom said brightly. "And the owner

was open to leasing or selling to the right person. Let's take a look."

Sarah had to make an effort to rein in the hope that filled her chest as they walked up the gravel pathway to the front door. She could see so much promise in the tattered flowers that had been destroyed in the storm, the little stone chimney that rose up from the right side of the cottage... This place was a true *home*, not just an apartment to retreat to for a snatch of privacy. It was more than just a place to sleep.

The cottage *did* need a lot of work – just on the outside, she could see boards that needed to be replaced and a gutter that was ready to drop off – but it looked like work she could do herself, with a little bit of help from Jeff.

As they reached the front door, it opened of its own accord. An old man gave them a level look, taking them in without immediately offering a greeting.

"Are you Mr. Henderson?" Steph asked brightly.

"That's me. You're here about the house?"

"We are. My name is Stephanie. We spoke on the phone."

"Which one of you is interested?"

"My daughter, Sarah."

"Hi." Sarah smiled uncertainly and raised her hand in a half wave. With his grizzled gray beard and flat stare, Mr. Henderson looked like a troll that she had to placate in order to gain access to this storybook place. He let the door open the rest of the way, and a white dog pushed past his legs.

"Hello there," Steph crooned. Sarah crouched down beside her mother, happy to have something to focus on besides Mr. Henderson's stormy expression. "I know you. You're Milo!"

The dog was a sweet old thing, some sort of mixed breed with a wiry white coat and a beard-like scruff on his chin. He licked Sarah's hands and pressed closer as they pet him, his whole body wagging from side to side in exuberant greeting. When Sarah risked a glance at Mr. Henderson, the man's face had softened considerably.

"How do you know Milo?" Mr. Henderson rumbled.

"I used to run the veterinary clinic downtown," Steph told him. "My son runs it now."

"Doctor Ketterman the second," Sarah chimed in.

"Your wife used to bring Milo in. It's been a while. I stitched up a pretty serious bite the last time I saw him, if memory serves. Yes, there it is." Steph parted Milo's coat to show a thick strip of skin with no hair growing on it. "It healed beautifully."

"Doberman wandered into our yard when I left the gate open," Mr. Henderson said. "Cornered Milo over there. Didn't let up until Edna went at him with a broom."

"How is Edna?" Steph asked, rising to her feet. Sarah stayed where she was, giving Milo a good scratch. He leaned against her, closing his eyes with pleasure.

"She passed away the year before last. Just after Christmas."

"I'm sorry to hear that," Steph said with genuine emotion. "She was lovely."

"She was a spitfire," Mr. Henderson said with a low chuckle. "And she was my whole life." He touched the door frame with a tenderness that bordered on a caress and said, "This was our first house together, and we made it our home again after our boys moved out and the other place felt too big. There are so many memories here that I couldn't hand the place over to just anyone. But Milo and I live down in Cherry Blossom Point now, with my younger son and his wife. Their kids keep us young. But I just can't maintain this place the way it deserves. The time in the car is hell on my back, and Milo gets car sick more often than not. He likes you," Mr. Henderson added suddenly.

Sarah met his eyes with a smile, gave Milo one last scratch between the ears, and stood. "He's a sweetheart."

"Not always." Mr. Henderson chuckled again. "Come on in."

The cottage had wooden floors worn soft with age. It was furnished with beautiful, understated antiques. Other than a new mattress to replace the creaking springs on the current one, Sarah wouldn't have to buy any furniture at all; the listing had said that the place was being offered fully furnished. The fireplace was made of stone, just like the chimney. The kitchen wasn't huge, but the farmhouse-style kitchen sink *was*. And there was just enough counter space to spread out and make pasta or pie crusts.

She loved it. Every last nook and corner of it.

Mr. Henderson had given them space to explore and chat about all the little details and the minor fixes that could be made by the time the weather turned cold. When they had seen everything there was to see, they found him standing in the backyard.

The yard was pocket sized, but the *view*... The view made Sarah stop mid-step on her way out the kitchen door. The cottage was situated on a slight rise, and she could see the whole horizon over her neighbor's roof. The beach was a mix of black rocks and soft sand, with tourists and locals out enjoying the summer day. She could hear the waves crashing against rock and sand from where she stood. If she left her bedroom windows open in summertime, the sound would lull her to sleep. And the sunrises from her little back porch – *the* porch, Sarah corrected herself quickly, *this* porch, not *her* porch – must be phenomenal.

She was trying not to get her hopes up, but she was already in love with this little cottage. This *home*. She could see herself living there, easy walking distance from one of her favorite beaches in the state. There was an endless list of home improvement projects that she could take on – and to Sarah's surprise, the idea of it felt like a pleasure rather than a chore. She tore her eyes away from the beach to take in the back of the cottage, picturing all of the things she could do to bring it back to its former glory.

"We used to have a hammock here," Mr. Henderson said softly, "between these two trees."

Sarah turned to him and sat down on the steps, scratching Milo's head as she listened.

"We used to lay here side by side watching the sunrise, planning out our life together. Where we would go when we had the money, what kinds of memories we wanted to create for our kids... and we accomplished nearly everything we dreamed of. And a whole lot more besides."

"It's...amazing," she replied sincerely as she blinked back the tears stinging her eyes.

The old man watched her silently and then offered her a watery smile. "Yeah, this feels good. I knew it the second Milo took to you. He's an excellent judge of character. Edna would've loved you. The place is yours if you want it, kiddo."

"I'll take it," Sarah said with uncharacteristic spontaneity. So maybe it wasn't the safe choice, with the sterile certainty of a new build and a warranty to go with it. Sarah didn't care. She loved it. She wanted it. She wanted a *home*.

"We can start with a lease," Mr. Henderson said. "And maybe if you decide you want to buy it down the line, we'll work something out. If not, I'll reimburse you for any repairs."

"Deal," Sarah said happily.

"Milo and I should be getting on the road so we can get home with plenty of time to spare. I can't see a thing driving after sundown. But we can drive back up this weekend with the papers, if you'd like to move in then."

"I would love to." Sarah loped down the stairs and shook the man's hand. "Thank you so much for trusting me with this home, Mr. Henderson. It's really something special."

He nodded, blinking back tears. "It really is."

Back in Steph's car, Sarah let out a squeal of glee. "I can't believe that place exists! I can't believe you found it!"

"Let's celebrate!" Steph said as she started the car. "There's a new seafood place on the wharf I've been wanting to try. What do you think?"

"I'm game," Sarah said happily. "Let's go. My treat."

The restaurant was lovely, with the windows on one side looking over the same stretch of beach that the little cottage – *Sarah's* cottage – had a view of. Her mind was already tumbling with the possibilities of her new life. Maybe this would be her new place. She could be a regular. She could bike here when the weather was this nice. She could buy a bike! Not a road bike like she'd had in DC but the sort of beach cruiser that she'd loved as a kid.

"I'm going to get the shrimp fettuccine," Steph said,

pulling Sarah out of her reverie. "What are you going to order?"

Sarah looked over the specials menu, the better part of her attention still on the life that she would create for herself on the magical piece of earth she had just claimed as her own.

"The black sea bass looks good. I've never had green papaya salad."

"Oh, I've had that in Thai restaurants. It's so tasty. They usually top it with peanuts, though," her mother said.

"I'll have the black sea bass," Sarah told the waitress when the girl came back for her order. "But can you tell me if there are any nuts in the dish?"

The girl scrunched her face and paused before shaking her head. "Nope, no nuts in that," she replied, punching the order into her handheld computer. "Anything to drink?"

Sarah and her mom were chatting about home improvement projects when their food came. Sarah's fish was tender and buttery; it went beautifully with the crunchy citrus flavor of the papaya salad. But just a few bites in, Sarah felt a telltale tingling sensation in her mouth. Her eyes started to burn, and her fingers were suddenly clumsy on her fork.

"Mom," she blurted. Steph stopped speaking mid-sentence and looked up from her food.

"Where's your purse?" she asked hurriedly. Without waiting for an answer, she snatched Sarah's bag up from under the table and looked through it frantically. After a moment of searching, she shoved her plate aside and dumped the purse out on the table. "Where is it?"

It was in her car, Sarah realized as blackness crept in at the edges of her vision. She reached futilely into the pockets of her lightweight summer jacket. I don't have it, she tried to tell her mom, but she couldn't get a full breath in.

The EpiPen that usually lived in her purse was still in the glove compartment of her car.

"Help!" Steph was just across the little table, but her voice sounded oddly distant. "Does anyone have an EpiPen? We need help!"

Sarah braced herself on the table to keep from falling out of her seat as her vision grew dark. Her throat constricted. Panic squeezed her lungs... She drew in one last painful, wheezing breath. There was a sudden, stabbing blow to her leg... and everything went black.

20

FALLYN

"So you're saying that Betty Carson is the next target, then?" David asked as he turned onto Blueberry Street in the neighborhood that they had been frequenting since the start of their investigation.

"I'd bet my life on it," Fallyn said, leaning forward in her seat to see the house numbers. It was nearly dark outside, but most of the houses in The Berries were well lit – especially after the recent robberies. Fallyn and David had interviewed the Ambergers regarding their missing valuables, and now they were driving by Betty Carson's place for a quick look.

It had taken some doing, but Fallyn and David had uncovered all of the names of the earliest adopters of the SkinniQuick pyramid scheme – the ones who had actually earned back their initial investment and then some by convincing enough people to join their "reverse funnel". Every single person who had been robbed was on that list.

This time, they had a little more to go on. The Ambergers had installed a security camera after the first neighborhood robbery, and the camera had captured an older woman walking past their house on the night before their valuables were stolen. It was only a few seconds, and she was far enough from the camera that she was a bit blurry, but it was something. She was a trim woman with gray hair, and she was carrying a leash. She might be the perpetrator... or for all they knew, she might just be a distant neighbor looking for her lost dog. But maybe she had seen something. It was worth looking into, at least.

"If this lead doesn't pan out," David droned, "we'll have to make a list of everyone who ever bought into the SkinniQuick down chain and go through them one by one."

"That would be a long list," Fallyn said wryly.

"Maybe Molly's our cat burglar," he joked.

Fallyn laughed. "You shut your mouth."

He parked across the street from Betty Carson's house and they gave it a long look. No different from the other houses that had been robbed. It was only a matter of time.

"We should warn her," Fallyn said.

"Doesn't look like anyone's home," David said. "But we will. I still have her number. It's back in my office, on the list that Charles gave me."

They had interviewed Betty briefly, back when they were still trying to figure out what set the victims' houses apart from the houses that had been passed over. Aside from Deirdre, Betty was the only person in the neighborhood that Fallyn had taken a genuine liking to. Apparently, her instincts about people weren't as sharp as they used to be.

"We should work with the cops to set up a sting operation," David said.

"A sting operation?" Fallyn repeated in a dry tone.

He nodded, eyes on Betty's house. "I'll get a complete list of people who might have been harmed by their scam and go through them one by one. In the meantime, the cops should keep someone posted on the Carson place in case the burglar shows up. Maybe Ms. Carson could be enticed to go on vacation for a while, after stashing her valuables elsewhere."

"A setup," Fallyn said.

"A sting operation," David said agreeably. He put the car in drive and moved down the street. "I'll head straight to the office, if that's alright with you. Start making some calls?"

"Sure," Fallyn murmured, distracted. There was a moving truck down the street. As they got closer, she realized that it was parked in front of Deirdre's house. "Didn't she have a few more months on her lease?"

"What's that?"

"Deirdre. Look, she's outside. Pull over, would you?"

David did as she asked. "Why are we stopping?"

"I just have a few more questions for her."

"All right. I'll stay here, if you don't mind, and start on those calls."

"Sure." Fallyn opened the passenger's side door, and Deirdre gave Fallyn a deer-in-the-headlights look as Fallyn stepped out of the car.

"Fallyn!" Deirdre gave her a somewhat nervous smile. "What are you doing here?"

"We just left the Amberger's place. You know they were robbed just this past week?"

"I hadn't heard." Deirdre glanced at her son, who was carrying an end table to the moving truck. "Thanks, Carter! Why don't you go put that pizza in the oven?"

"Okay, Mom." He loped back into the house.

"I didn't realize you were moving out so soon!" Fallyn tried to keep her voice light and friendly. "How's it going so far?"

"Oh, fine. Moving's never easy. I figured we'd get a jump on it, get all settled in before the next school year starts, you know?"

"Sure, that makes sense," Fallyn said... even though it was still early in the summer, and Deirdre would be paying the rent on this place for a good while yet. Fallyn gave way to her instincts and took a wild leap. "Did you know that all of the victims of the robberies were high-level officers in a multi-level marketing business about ten years ago?"

"You mean a pyramid scheme," Deirdre said sharply. Then, she paled. If Fallyn had hoped to get a reaction from her blunt delivery, she wasn't disappointed. Deirdre swallowed and looked away. Fallyn held her tongue as Carter came back out with another big moving box and shoved it into the truck.

"Oven's preheating," he announced happily.

"Thanks." Deirdre's voice sounded weak and shaky, but her son didn't seem to notice. He was already headed back inside. She turned back to Fallyn and asked softly, "Would you like to come inside for a glass of lemonade?"

Fallyn nodded and followed her across the lawn, knowing that something big was about to happen. Deirdre didn't even keep up the pretense of lemonade – just led her straight into the living room and slumped into one corner of her cushy sofa.

"Are you close with your parents, Fallyn?"

That was unexpected. Fallyn let out a quick breath

through her nose as she sat down at the opposite end of the couch. Why did that question keep coming up? She responded with a one-shouldered shrug and a shake of her head. "Not particularly."

"I am," Deirdre said quietly. "My mom and dad are... they're my people, you know? My heroes, my biggest fans, my steady support system since... always. They worked so hard to give me all of the things that they never had growing up. Stability and love and the freedom to do what made me happy. When my husband took off on me five years into my marriage, I moved back in with my parents until I found my footing again. Even when I got a house of my own, they were always there for me. My dad's been a father to Carter in every way that matters."

Fallyn nodded along, just letting Deirdre talk.

The other woman's eyes were distant as she continued, "Imagine spending your whole life saving and scrimping to retire, and finally being able to do it, and do it in style. In an amazing house you could never hope to afford until late in life. Going on the vacations you'd dreamed of for decades. They used to talk about putting Carter through college..." She shook her head and turned to look Fallyn in the eyes. "They lost everything when they moved here. There was a neighborhood party thrown just to pitch the pyramid scheme to the new neighbors, and my parents bought into it. Here were all of these uber-rich people telling them that this new company was a sure thing... and they trusted them."

Deirdre paused and took a deep, steadying breath. She continued in a tone of painstaking calm. "Everyone who had sold them on it rebounded just fine when the whole scheme came crashing down. They all had deep pockets. Family money, other investments... But it destroyed my parents. They lost their home just months after buying it. They lost their dignity. They moved in with Carter and me for a while, which would have been fine... but my dad was so ashamed. He ended up working nights as a janitor, because it was the only thing he could find. Then, he got laid off from *that* job and he just spiraled. He felt so guilty for losing their savings, so low over what he saw as an inability to provide..."

Deirdre was silent for a long moment. Again, Fallyn waited her out.

"I found him just in time," Deirdre said at last. Her eyes were glassy, and her voice shook. "He had closed himself into the garage, started the car... he was unconscious, but he was still alive. I called the ambulance... He felt so terrible, when he came to. So guilty. When I think of him in that hospital bed with tears going down his face... ugh. It just guts me. Every time."

"I'm sorry," Fallyn said quietly, infusing the words with the genuine sympathy that she felt for Deirdre and her family. What kind of people would trick a retired couple out of everything they had? And for what? The people behind the scheme had been so wealthy already.

"I was so angry," Deirdre said, though there was nothing but desolation in her voice.

Fallyn felt a growing horror, an impulse to run from the house before Deirdre said something that she regretted... but she sat rooted to the spot, fascinated by the tale that was unfolding.

"Someone needed to pay," Deirdre continued, her eyes

fixed somewhere in middle distance. "I just wanted to take back what was rightfully theirs. Just enough from everyone involved to replenish my parents' life savings and give them the golden years that they deserve. And I did it. I'm done," she said with quiet desperation, looking back to Fallyn. "Everyone has paid. I just want to walk away and call it even. Move on with my life. Help my parents move on with theirs."

She pulled out her phone and fiddled with it for a moment, then handed it to Fallyn with a sorrowful smile. "I just put an offer in on this house. Ocean view. My mom will love that."

Fallyn looked at the real estate listing, not really seeing it. Her stomach churned with a confused mix of emotions. What Deirdre had done was illegal, but there was a clear justice to it – albeit justice of the vigilante variety. There was a roar of questions going through her mind, and she could have laughed at the absurdity of which one came tumbling out first.

"Why did you rob Charles twice?"

Deirdre *did* laugh. "I only robbed him once. The second time was probably insurance fraud, after he saw how much he got the first time around. Most of them probably didn't lose *any* money," she added sourly. "The rich know how to hang on to their ill-gotten gains."

Fallyn thought back to her conversation with Charles Ericson. What had he claimed was stolen the second time? Some exorbitantly priced whiskey. Had the devious troll simply enjoyed his whisky and then claimed it as another casualty of the neighborhood robberies?

"What about Betty Carson?" Fallyn asked.

"What about her?" Deirdre shot back.

"She was one of them, wasn't she?"

Deirdre's eyebrows rose. "Wow. You really did your homework." She sighed. "Truth is? Betty was the only person in the neighborhood who was genuinely kind to us when we moved in. She brought us a housewarming gift, invited me to join the neighborhood book club, spent the whole evening chatting with me when the others gave me the cold shoulder... She's hard not to like. I think she's genuinely a good person."

"I got that impression too."

"Either she's changed, or she didn't realize what she was getting into with the pyramid scheme. I'm not a monster, Fallyn."

"Pizza's ready!" Carter called from the kitchen. Fallyn watched a kaleidoscope of emotions flash across Deirdre's face...pride and hope and fear and grief. Fallyn felt a similar tumult of emotions at the knowledge that if she turned Deirdre in, she would be ruining not only Deirdre's life, but also that of her son..

"I know it was wrong," the other woman said softly with a shake of her head. "I knew it about halfway through, but I was already in so deep. I needed to see it through, and I had myself convinced that it was a victimless crime. Wasn't it?" she asked, looking Fallyn full in the face, clearly searching for absolution. "Those people aren't victims. They're predators. I didn't ruin their lives. I didn't do anything besides give them a bit of a scare. They didn't lose much of anything, really. It's not true justice. It's just enough to make things right for my mom and dad."

"What about the maid who was fired?" Fallyn pressed.

She frowned at the amusement that flashed across Deirdre's face. "What about the spouses who weren't even around for the SkinniQuick debacle, who don't feel safe in their own homes now?"

"They're just as bad as the people they're married to, and you know it. And I *was* the maid."

"What?" Fallyn was shocked. "How good are you at disguises?"

Deirdre snorted. "You don't need to be good. People like that don't look at the help. Not really. They didn't even see me."

Fallyn looked out the window. Other questions flashed through her head, about how Deirdre had pulled all of this off, how she had learned to crack safes... they were questions that Fallyn didn't actually want the answers to.

She already knew too much.

She could see David outside in his car, still talking on the phone.

What was she going to tell him?

"I understand what you need to do," Deirdre said quietly. "If I could do it all over again, I never would have come back here. I would have found another way. But what's done is done. I won't run from it."

She stood, and Fallyn followed her lead. As she opened the front door, Deirdre said, "I wish we could have met under better circumstances, Fallyn. We might have been friends... and maybe you would have been able to talk me out of this."

Deirdre offered her a wry smile, but there was a deep grief in her eyes. Fallyn wanted to assure her that she was safe...that she wouldn't hand this lovely woman in just to salve the bruised egos of a handful of unpleasant people.

But she couldn't.

Not yet.

She needed time to reflect on it, away from Deirdre's son and her charm. She needed time to think.

Fallyn said her goodbyes and walked back to the car, stomach churning like a summer storm.

21

SARAH

"The place should be shut down." Steph's voice was ragged. "Anna, my God, she almost–"

Sarah forced her eyes open, blinking the grit away. Her face still felt tender and her throat was raw, but she was mostly back to normal. She looked up to find her mother standing beside her bed, or more accurately, Todd's couch, biting back tears.

"I'm okay, Mom," she managed with a tired smile. She wondered if her mom had gone home the night before. Had she slept at all? Steph had been at Sarah's side last night when she fell asleep, and she was still there now. Sarah sought for something that she could say to assuage her mom's anxieties. "In fact, once I have a good, strong cup of coffee, I'll be right as rain. Can you go make me a cup?"

Stephanie nodded wordlessly, as if she didn't trust herself to speak, and then padded out of the room, leaving Aunt Anna behind.

"Oh, peanut, you gave your poor mama a real scare last night," she murmured, leaning in and pressing a cool hand to

Sarah's brow. "I had to talk her off the ledge. She was about ready to head back to that restaurant, toss a Molotov cocktail through the window, and set that whole place on fire."

This got a chuckle out of Sarah as she tried to imagine her mother doing such a thing.

"Apparently, the poor waitress took an ambulance right after you. She had a panic attack. It was her third day on the job and she had no idea what she'd done," Anna continued. Sarah sat up and pulled her blankets into a heap to make room for her aunt, who sat down beside her on the couch. That poor waitress.

"She was sweet," Sarah said, "and I don't want her to lose her job or anything…"

Anna nodded. "I get it, but she really has to understand how serious allergies can be. The restaurant owner promised he would require all new staff to take a short online course on the subject going forward."

"That's good."

"Who ordered a cup of joe?" Todd boomed as he walked into the room. He had a tendency to balance out their mom's anxiety with overenthusiastic good cheer.

Just like Dad.

Sarah swallowed the tears that rose at the thought of her father. When she was sure that she had control over her voice, she stood up and said to her brother, "Thank you, but you don't need to bring me breakfast on the couch. I'd rather come into the kitchen."

"As you desire, my liege," Todd said, bowing and scraping.

Sarah laughed in spite of herself. "Stop it. Give me my coffee before you spill it."

"Your Aunt Anna brought us a feast," Steph said as they walked in. She was laying out the food as she spoke. Anna had brought them a silly number of bagels and a rainbow array of different flavors of cream cheese from Sarah's favorite breakfast place.

Sarah gave her aunt a one-armed hug, still clutching her coffee in her other hand. "Thank you. I'm starved."

"I hear you turned your nose up at your dinner last night," Todd said. "Always so high maintenance."

"Ha ha," she said flatly.

"Sit down, Sarah." Steph pulled out Sarah's chair for her, still fluttering anxiously around the kitchen. "I'll get you your food."

Sarah did as she was told. She didn't usually appreciate this sort of coddling – but truth be told, she still wasn't feeling a hundred percent after that shock to her system the night before. She'd be okay soon, though. Bagels and coffee should do the trick.

From the other side of the kitchen, Anna gave her a look that said, *Mothers. What can you do?*

"Sweet or savory?" Steph asked.

"Did I see their strawberry cream cheese?" Sarah asked with a smile. "And the cinnamon sugar bagels?"

"Coming right up!"

Clutching her own oversized coffee mug, Anna took a seat at the kitchen table beside Sarah. "I was up at dawn to get all the best flavors."

Sarah chuckled. "You were not."

"I was. Waited two hours in the snow to be first in line."

"Aunt Anna, it's summertime."

"Fought a bear on my way out," Anna said solemnly.

"She went right for the cinnamon sugar bagels, but I wouldn't let her have one. 'Those are for my niece,' I told her."

Sarah ceased her protests and let Anna spin her stories while she bit into a chewy bagel topped with whipped strawberry cream cheese. It was divine, and she felt stronger the moment she swallowed the first bite.

Her family calmed somewhat when they sat down to eat their own bagels, slowly shifting from crisis mode back into their usual family dynamics. Todd was entertaining their mom and aunt with some story about Barnaby the parrot that Sarah couldn't be bothered to follow. Half of her attention was on her scrumptious breakfast. And the other half? Was wrestling with the momentous decisions that she had to make this week.

Well. She had a place to live. That was one major thing off the list.

And the rest of it?

Sarah couldn't help but think about all of the things she'd been worried about, all the time and energy that she had wasted second-guessing her every choice. Why *should* she play it safe all the time? She hadn't done that with her new home. She'd seen something she loved and she had jumped on it. And that had felt so good. It felt right.

She was ready to make the leap on her other decisions too.

A near-death experience could really give a girl a bit of a different perspective. She had to stop being afraid to fail – because who knew what tomorrow might bring? If she had left her earthly body for good last night, what were the things she would have regretted?

She could feel her strength returning with each bite of

food, and her resolve strengthening along with it. The moment she'd finished her last bite of bagel, she pushed her chair away from the table and stood.

"Sarah?" her mom asked, immediately on edge again. "Are you okay?"

"I'm fine." Sarah smiled at her mom, trying to reassure her. "I'm great. I just have a couple of phone calls to make. I'll be right back."

Todd gave her a suspicious look, but Aunt Anna saved her with a wave of her hand. "Earth to Todd! What happened once you'd wrangled Barnaby into your Jeep?"

Sarah walked outside and closed the door behind her. The morning sunshine was warm on her face, and she closed her eyes for the space of a few heartbeats, giving thanks for the day. The fresh air moving in and out of her lungs was no small thing. She was profoundly grateful just to be breathing. Everything else was frosting on the cupcake.

After a moment, she opened her eyes and unlocked her phone. Her heart was pounding now. Nerves, excitement... it was impossible to untangle the two.

"Just rip it off like a Band-Aid," she murmured as the phone rang. The moment the call connected, she jumped in with both feet. "Hi, this is Sarah Sullivan. I just wanted to thank you again for the offer, but I'm calling to let you know that I'm going to be pursuing other opportunities."

"Okay, Sarah. Thank you for following up."

"Of course. You have a good day," she said, feeling sort of silly but unsure of how to end the call.

"You too, Sarah. And if you change your mind or decide to go in a different direction in the future, please don't hesitate to reapply."

"I will. I mean, I won't. Hesitate. Thank you!" Sarah hung up before she made more of a fool of herself. Despite her decidedly imperfect stumbling, she was grinning so much that her cheeks ached. On to the next item. Sarah sat down on the front step and started typing.

Hi Val! I've been thinking about your job offer and I'm interested in hearing more. I had an allergic reaction to something with peanuts yesterday and I'm still recovering but I'd love to meet up and talk about it more if you're free sometime this week?

Three dots appeared almost immediately as Val began to type her reply. Sarah felt a thread of nervousness. She probably should have turned down the other job *after* sitting down to a meeting with Val. But no. What would be the point of that?

She could do this. She *would* do this. She was all in.

Hi Sarah! I'm so happy to hear from you. I'm sorry to hear that you had an allergic reaction, but I'm so excited for our meeting! I'm free at lunchtime any day after tomorrow. Let me know when you're feeling one hundred percent and we can talk over lunch, if that works for you?

Sarah might have shouted in glee if she wasn't wary of bringing her whole family out to check on her. Instead, she pumped her fist in the air and texted back, *Sounds good!*

Now for the hard part...

She typed a quick text to Adam and sent it before she could second-guess herself or overthink what she was doing. All it said was, *Can we talk?*

Delivered, said the fine print below her text.

And then, a moment later, *Read.*

She waited. No dot-dot-dot. No reply.

She waited a while longer, watching a squirrel race up a nearby tree.

And then, she stopped waiting. So he saw it and didn't reply. So what? He was probably working. Anyway, she wasn't the type to sit by the phone waiting for a call. Or a text…

Sarah walked straight through to the bathroom. She was still wearing her clothes from yesterday and she felt like death warmed over, so she took a quick shower and threw on some clean clothes before rejoining her family in the kitchen.

"Ready for a savory bagel?" Steph asked the moment she saw her.

Sarah chuckled. "Sure. But don't get up. Please. I'll get it." She helped herself to a sesame bagel with sun-dried tomato cream cheese and reclaimed the seat next to Anna. She was telling Steph and Todd about her flying lessons, but Sarah's attention was just as scattered as before. She kept checking her phone… Nothing. Her appetite was gone, but she mechanically chewed her bagel to placate her mom.

Had she scared him off already? Had he lost interest and moved on to someone else? Probably. She had manifested exactly what she'd feared by pushing him away over and over again.

"Are you saying you don't trust me?" Anna's voice rose in mock outrage, and Steph laughed.

"Not enough to get on one of those tiny planes with you."

"I'm shocked and offended." She actually sounded like she was trying not to laugh.

"Remember the go cart?"

Now, Anna did laugh. "I was eight!"

"Never. Again."

Sarah looked at her phone again without even thinking about what she was doing. Then, she saw Todd watching her.

"Whose call are you sweating?" he asked with a frown.

Sarah blinked back a few foolish tears. "It doesn't matter."

Todd's face softened, which only made her more embarrassed. She was still overwrought from the night before, that was all. So what if he couldn't be bothered to text her back? She had big plans on the horizon! She didn't –

Sarah's half-hearted hype speech was interrupted by the doorbell. Todd went to answer it, and they heard the murmur of lowered voices for a minute before Todd walked back in. He gave Sarah a narrow-eyed look, and she raised her eyebrows in response.

Then, Adam walked in. He was carrying a gift basket that took two hands to hold. At the front of the haul was a card that said *Feel better soon!*

"Hello there!" Anna said emphatically.

Todd rolled his eyes; Sarah glanced at him and looked back to Adam with a grin.

"I guess we'll leave you two to talk," Todd said with a sigh.

"Yes," Anna agreed. "Please, don't let us get in your way!"

Steph stood, looking from Sarah to Adam and back again with wide eyes. Anna gave her a gentle shove towards the door, grinning all the while like the Cheshire cat.

Sarah's cheeks burned as her family filed out of the room, but she felt her smile grow wider as she looked at Adam and his ungainly gift basket.

"You didn't have to do all that," she said as he set it on the table in front of her.

"How are you feeling?" He turned Anna's recently vacated chair so that it was facing Sarah and sat down, leaning towards her with his arms braced on his knees.

"I'm fine," Sarah said, still blushing. The intense way he was staring at her wasn't giving her any space to regain her composure. "It's nothing that hasn't happened before."

"I was planning to bring your car back today anyway, and then I heard what had happened. I just wanted to check in. I was in the gift shop when your message came through." He grinned a grin that made her stomach do somersaults. "You wanted to talk?"

She nodded and swallowed hard, trying to work up the nerve to explain what was on her mind.

"What did you want to talk about?" he pressed in a gentle tone. The purr of his voice did nothing to calm her nerves, but she pressed forward all the same.

"I wanted to explain that I've come to realize some things over the past few weeks, but especially last night. I had a moment of clarity when I found my new house, and then the whole near-death experience thing..." Sarah laughed weakly, trying to make light of it, but Adam's expression was unusually serious. She had his undivided attention.

"I was always a bit of a control freak," she admitted. "A perfectionist, driven to succeed, all of those things. But when my dad died–" Sarah's voice broke, and she paused. Took a deep breath. Pressed on. "When I lost my dad, things got worse. It was like an obsession. I couldn't control the most important things in my life, so I *had* to control the things that I *could* control. Does that make sense?"

Adam nodded, green eyes intent on her face.

"I got to the point that I wouldn't allow myself to take any risks or put myself out there for fear of adding to my pile of sadness and heartache. You were one of the things I was afraid of," she admitted quietly. "I know I probably seem ridiculously fickle and if you don't want to put up with that, then I totally get it but–"

Adam took both of Sarah's hands in his, and she stopped talking.

"Your Honor," he said with a touch of his usual good humor, "I was already preparing to file my appeal when you texted me."

A smile pulled at the sides of her mouth as she looked into his eyes. "Oh yeah?"

"Did you think I was just going to let you walk away?" Adam was smiling, but there was a rough emotion to his voice. "You are so beautiful, Sarah. And you keep me on my toes. When I'm with you, I feel *here*. I feel alive. And if you take a chance on me, well... I promise to be worth the risk."

Sarah melted, leaning forward until the space between them disappeared. She lost track of time, lost all sense of anything happening beyond her and Adam – until her Aunt Anna cut in with a wolf whistle.

"Sorry guys," she said brightly, sounding not sorry at all. "I forgot my mimosa."

Adam laughed. "It's alright. You can come in. I'll behave."

They stood, and he wrapped an arm around Sarah's shoulders. Nestling into the nook of his shoulder felt so unexpectedly comfortable.

It felt right.

"Mimosas all around!" she declared as Todd and Steph came cautiously back into the kitchen. "I want to celebrate my new cottage, and my new job." She didn't say, *"And my new boyfriend!",* but she did wrap an arm around Adam's waist as she spoke. She shot Todd a challenging look; he responded with a shrug and a smile.

"To new beginnings," Anna said, handing them each a glass of champagne and orange juice.

"To starting over," Sarah added. "To starting over here in Bluebird Bay, surrounded by the people I care about most."

22

FALLYN

"Fallyn, sweetheart? You have a visitor!"

She looked away from the rain streaming down the window as Molly's voice tugged her from her reverie.

David.

She'd been dreading this conversation and had hoped to put it off even longer by going diving solo, but the rain had killed that plan. There was no putting it off any longer.

After they'd left The Berries yesterday, she'd been a total head case. On the car ride back to his office, David had tried to fill her in on what he had learned from his phone calls, but it had been like a low-level buzzing in her ears. All she could think about was Deirdre and her story. She was ready to leap out of the car and run the rest of the way back to the inn so she could deep dive on the internet and maybe disprove what Deirdre had told her. Instead, she'd unearthed enough background on the parties involved to be fully convinced the woman had been telling the truth.

Which left her in a terrible, awful predicament.

On one hand, David had been hired to root out the cat burglar, and she was working for him. The logical thing to do would be to tell him what she'd learned, close the case up nice and tight, and collect the fee plus the bonus.

But for the past two days, logic had been in a fight to the death against empathy. And so far?

Empathy was winning the battle.

"Be right there!" she called down to Molly as she paused in front of the mirror.

Yup, she looked exactly like she felt. Someone who had been through the ringer struggling with an existential crisis for the past day and a half.

As she made her way to the lobby, she was no closer to a decision than she had been at the start. David's slow-building smile didn't make her dilemma any easier to manage. Keeping this information from him felt like such a betrayal of trust, all to protect someone, a criminal that she barely knew. But if she *did* tell him what she knew, and he felt obligated to take that information to the authorities? The consequences for Deirdre and her family would be so, so much worse than David not getting his reward money. Carter would be left without a mother. He still had his grandparents... but considering how badly Deirdre's father had taken his financial mishaps in the past, seeing his daughter imprisoned as a direct result of his mistakes would most likely be too much for the old man to bear.

And too much guilt for Fallyn to carry.

She realized David had said something that hadn't registered, and that his smile had morphed into a look of concern at her lack of response.

"Fallyn? Are you all right?"

"Sure." She gave him a smile that was no less genuine for all of the worry behind it. Because beneath all the worry, she felt deeply touched that he cared.

"Are you hungry, David?" Molly asked. She was in her armchair behind the front desk, Kindle in hand. "Fallyn hardly touched her food this morning. There's plenty left."

"I just ate, fool that I am." David's voice was a low rumble that Fallyn could feel in her stomach. The man had such a solid presence to him. No wonder he still reminded her of old movies.

"Well, you tell me if you get hungry later." Molly's eyes had already drifted back to her novel.

"Thank you." David looked at Fallyn and raised his eyebrows. She led him up the stairs to her room, still going round in circles in her mind. If the stakes were the same for both parties, she would be loyal to a friend over a stranger. But that wasn't the case here. It just *wasn't*. Oh, but still. Didn't David deserve to know? She had to tell him. He'd been nothing but a friend to her. Hell, who was she kidding? He was more than that – he could be a *lot* more than that, if she let him – and there was no way she was going to lie to him more than she already had. Even this lie of omission was souring her stomach. She needed to come clean to him about why she had gone to talk to Deirdre and about everything the woman had said... But how would he react?

Fallyn took a deep breath as she closed the door to her room and turned to face him.

Only one way to find out.

She just had to trust him... and hope that she knew him as well as she thought she did.

"I'm off the case," David said without preamble, crossing the room to sit in the window seat.

"What?" Fallyn trailed after him, surprised out of her worry spiral. She sat on the bench beside him. The seat was small enough that her knee brushed against his.

"I just got the call. I've been fired from the cat burglar case."

"I'm sorry to hear that," she said in a soft voice. Lying through her teeth.

"I'm not." David smiled. "More time for diving. And they were an unpleasant bunch. I don't need the money, not really. It would have been... I don't know, fun money. I thought I might coax you to take a trip with me."

Fallyn looked down, half hiding the smile and blush that lit up her face at his words. *Stay on target*, she told herself.

"I think we could still manage that," she murmured. "But first, I have a... hypothetical question to ask you."

"Oh?"

"About the case. I've been wanting to talk to you about something."

"Shoot."

"If someone had been wronged... or if a great wrong was done to the people they love... and the only way to make it right was to steal that money back from the thieves..." Fallyn cleared her throat. How could she pose a hypothetical without giving away the truth of it all? She pressed on. "If the person wasn't a threat to society, if they were a good person who definitely wouldn't reoffend, and they had people depending on them... All that hypothetically speaking, how would you handle that as a private investigator?"

"Hypothetically speaking?" David's voice was even, but

Fallyn thought she could see a glimmer of humor in his eyes. "I would suggest that the person in possession of this information didn't share it with me, as I would have a duty to report those findings to my client. But as long as I didn't know about it, well. I couldn't be implicated for concealing it."

Fallyn held back the smile that pulled at the corners of her mouth, afraid to get too excited. In a cautious tone, she asked, "And what about the reward money?"

David tilted his head, looking deep into Fallyn's eyes. "Sometimes money isn't the greatest reward."

"Right." Now, Fallyn did let her smile loose. Justice had been done, and they didn't have to undo it. A family was saved, and a good woman would walk free. And best of all?

David Shaw was exactly the man she thought he was. A man after her own heart, who valued people over money or career gains. A good man who was exactly what he seemed to be.

She kissed him quickly, before her nerves could get the better of her. He was still with shock for a fraction of a second, and then his arms were around her.

The kiss lasted a long while. When they finally came up for air, there was more joy on David's face than she had ever seen there before. He rested his forehead against hers and asked, "Does this mean that you've finally agreed to go into business with me for real?"

"Sure," Fallyn said, half laughing. "I really like...working with you."

She lost her nerve and changed course at the last minute, and David knew it. Oh well. There would be enough time for all of that. And David Shaw was a patient man.

"I love Bluebird Bay," she said in a steadier tone. "I love

the people here, and I love this inn too, but I'm ready to look for something more permanent."

"I'm so glad to hear that."

David kissed her, and she felt a whole world of promise in that kiss. But she wanted to take this slow and steady, just as they had done up until now, letting their friendship grow slowly... and slowly grow into something more.

She leaned back slightly and asked, "Do you want to stay a while? I was about to turn on a Golden Girls marathon. I'll even share my loot with you."

"There's no need to resort to bribery," he teased, "but I'm intrigued."

Fallyn crossed over to her dresser and pulled out a box of miniature Charleston Chews.

"Excellent," he said approvingly.

Fallyn chuckled and turned on the TV, then cuddled up next to David. Midway through the first episode, her phone rang. She was about to silence it when she saw who it was. So did David.

"You can answer it." He muted the TV. "Though, I may die of curiosity, never finding out how Blanche's date went."

Fallyn laughed and paused the show. David's eyebrows shot up.

"What is this sorcery?"

"Hello?" Fallyn had already answered the phone, so she bit back another laugh.

"Hey there, Fallyn. I'm sorry it took me so long to get back to you, but it was worth the wait."

She looked at David and held the phone away from her ear so he could hear, too. "Yeah?"

"According to my source, the three coins that you found

are part of the Lopez treasure that was lost in the mid eighteenth century. Each one is worth nearly five grand. If you can find the rest of it, well. That would be crazy money. Tens of millions."

"Thank you," Fallyn said, her voice blank with shock as she tried to get her head around what she was hearing. "I appreciate it."

"My pleasure! It's not every day a treasure like that comes through my shop. It's enough to make a man take up scuba diving."

"Yeah." Fallyn's eyes were fixed on David's face, but she was only half seeing him. She said her goodbyes and hung up. And then she kissed David Shaw again.

"Forget being private investigators," David laughed. "Let's go diving every day."

"Are you kidding?" Fallyn asked. "Because I would. I will. If I get a buyer for the coins, that could tide us over. Enough to go diving nearly every day for the rest of this summer."

"That sounds like a dream come true," David said, closing his hand around hers, "treasure or no treasure."

There was a knock on the door, and Fallyn went to open it.

"I'm sorry to interrupt," Molly said in a tone that hovered between prim and mischievous, "but you have another visitor. You're very popular today."

Fallyn and David exchanged a confused look. They walked down the stairs to find a soaking wet Cee-cee standing by the door, looking pale and scared.

"Cee-cee!" Fallyn exclaimed, hurrying down the last of the steps. "What's wrong?"

She gave Fallyn a miserable look, paused, and then let it all out in a rush...

"I think my ex-husband may have had something to do with Emily Addison's murder."

Did you enjoy Finding Comfort? Look for Finding Purpose, coming in March!

Want to get an alert next time a new book is out, find out about sales or contests, and chat with Christine? Join the mailing list **here!**

Maeve's Girls
(Standalone Women's Fiction)

Bluebird Bay
Finding Tomorrow
Finding Home
Finding Peace
Finding Forever
Finding Forgiveness
Finding Acceptance
Finding Redemption
Finding Refuge
Finding Comfort

Cherry Blossom Point
Starting From Scratch
Just Getting Started
A Fresh Start
A Head Start

Lucky Strickland Series (Mystery/Thriller)
Lucky Break

Crow's Feet Coven (Paranormal Women's Fiction)
Writing Wrongs
Brewing Trouble
Stealing Time

Made in United States
Troutdale, OR
03/03/2025